Modeled After Trouble

By:
T.M. DeLawrence

For my family...

Thank you for your encouragement and your support.

———————

She softly drummed her fingers along the steering wheel as the trumpets blared from the radio. Despite the reason for her travel throughout the countryside, she could feel her soul in harmony with the jazz band. She savored every note and chord that her ears could attend, dismissing what had transpired and the duty she was called upon to perform. The jazz music revived her joy for life while adding a colorful personality to the serene countryside setting. It made the perfect companion for her drive.

A gurgle from the passenger seat reminded her that she already had the perfect companion traveling with her. He playfully raised his hands high in the air and voiced his approval of his mother's choice of music. Her heart melted. He was the youngest of five children and seemed to be the only one who shared his mother's love for jazz.

She looked in the rear view mirror to find a blurred image of a car in the distance. She returned her focus on the road as she passed the sign that warned of sharp curves ahead. Her fingers tightened around the steering wheel as she reminded herself the number of accidental deaths that occurred on this part of the journey. She glanced at her baby boy confirming that he was bounded in the baby chair and that the chair was in no position to slide back and forth.

Confident that all was secured; she lowered her speed by five miles. Again, she glanced in her rearview mirror and found that the blurred image had focused into a sports car. It was quickly closing in on them. Obviously, the driver was defying the posted speed limit. In the back of her mind, she worried and prayed for the reckless youth. They would soon pass her and put their life in jeopardy, as did the others before them. They alone would have to face the consequences of their actions.

Another gurgle distracted her from the rearview mirror. She looked over to find that he was still fascinated with the jazz echoing through the car. She smiled and returned her sights on the road in front of her as she began her journey through the winding road.

As she rounded the first bend, she looked into the rear view mirror to find the sky behind her. A moment went by and soon the sports car was behind her and beginning its own treacherous journey. She tightened her grip around the steering wheel. She hoped the driver of the sports car would not include them in their blatant attempt to end their life unnecessarily. So often along this road, innocent drivers would be injured or killed because of another's negligence.

She checked her speed to ensure that she was not recklessly endangering herself and her baby. A sharp horn from behind snapped her head up to the rearview mirror. The sports car was now bearing down upon her. Her heart quickened as she began asking herself if something could be wrong with her car. It would explain the excessive speed of the sports car that had appeared in the distance and quickly made its way behind them.

The rim shots and the trumpets lowered as she adjusted the radio dial. She strained to hear anything out of the ordinary. She wondered if she was driving with a flat tire. She also looked around to see if there was any smoke coming from anywhere or if something was hanging off the car. Her response was nothing. The car seemed to look and operate within normal expectations.

Her head quickly jerked back as she heard the crunching of metal against metal. She gasped as the car slightly skidded around a curve. Her heart thumped wildly against her chest as she looked into the rearview mirror. She could see the sports car quickly closing in on her rear bumper.

A yelp escaped her lips as the tires screeched along the pavement. Her head again jerked back and she realized that her life was in jeopardy. She lowered her foot on the accelerator, hoping to put some distance between her and the sports car. She looked over at her baby and realized how imperative it was to accomplish that task.

She glanced in the rearview mirror to find the sports car coming in for another attack. She braced for impact as she rounded another curve. She could hear glass from the taillights smashing as the sports car forcefully connected with its target. She fought to maintain control of the steering wheel as she felt the rear end of the car swing out.

Tears flowed from her eyes as the tires clawed for traction. She compensated and re-took control of the car. She screamed as her head jerked again. She looked into the mirror frantically. The sports car seemed to be pushing her along the dangerous curves of the countryside.

She applied the brakes. The tires squealed as her back end slightly fishtailed back and forth. The sports car backed off a few yards and suddenly charged at her. The impact knocked her hands off the steering wheel and the car swerved uncontrollably towards the guardrail.

She screamed as she broke through the metal barrier. She could see the ground below as she bounced down the mountain. She looked at her baby as tears rolled down her eyes. This would be the last time she would see him. He gurgled once. He was too innocent to be aware of the fate that awaited them.

She grabbed onto the steering wheel and stomped on the brake, for whatever good it would do, as they picked up speed. She looked up at the windshield to find the massive trunk of a large tree in front of them. She could feel the car veering to the side. Maybe she would miss the tree. Her question was quickly answered when she heard the windshield and door window shatter as her side of the dashboard suddenly jumped out at her. The steering wheel slammed hard against her head and her scenery abruptly went black.

Her vision was blurred as she opened her eyes. She could smell the oil and gasoline that had spilt from the car. Her vision slowly cleared as she looked over at her traveling companion. His side of the car had been spared. He sat in the passenger seat and raised his hands with a slight yell of contentment. She gave a slight smile of relief realizing that he had came away from the accident unscathed.

The sound of a door closing quickly diverted her attention. She could hear footsteps crunching on the grass coming down the hill. Maybe someone had seen what happened and were coming to help. She reached for her seatbelt, but could not twist her arm or her body to unlock it. She was trapped.

"Help me!" she cried out with a cough. She felt like she was in a vice that tightened with every breath she took.

The footsteps came closer. She struggled to get free, but every attempt sent a sharp pain to her midsection. She looked over at her baby boy who had begun playing with his bonnet. She had to get him to safety if it was the last thing she did.

"Somebody please!" She cried out. "Help me and my baby!"

The footsteps came to a halt by the passenger door. She looked over to find a familiar face peering into the car. Her heart slowed realizing that she and her baby son would soon be free and their ordeal would be over.

"Thank GOD it's you," she said in relief. "Please help me. Please help me and my baby."

The would-be Samaritan looked down at the baby, took his gloved finger and tickled him along the rib cage. The little boy giggled as he squirmed about in the baby chair. He stopped and sighed. She could hear the regret that it carried. Again, she pleaded.

"Will you please help us?"

The familiar figure withdrew a gun. "I'm afraid I can't do that." and he fired once.

She saw the flash and felt quick prick against the middle of her chest immediately thereafter. She found herself beginning to lean backwards as her scenery began to fade away. Her last image was her son still in the baby chair. The jazz music echoed softly as he gurgled and gabbed baby talk. He raised his hands in appreciation of the music and his mother's fancy. His innocence was so invigorating. She fought to pray one last time that he would stay that way forever. She drifted off into a shroud of darkness before she could finish.

The figure stood atop the ridge and lit a cigarette. He exhaled a trail of smoke as the car below exploded into a huge ball of fire. He took another drag as he watched the car burn. He released another trail of smoke before he took in a deep breath. He knew there would be repercussions for his act, though the means of how he carried out his assignment was his decision alone. For a brief instant, he felt regret for his actions.

He quickly dismissed the emotion and quickly took one last toke from the cigarette. He then flicked it over the guardrail and blew a thin white stream of smoke. He quickly slid into the sports car and ignited the engine.

He had no time to be sentimental. He did what he was paid to do and there was still much work to be done. There was no room for regret or triumph. He did his job and that was all that was required of him. It was a job that had no room for emotion. It was a job in which he was considered a professional at. He maneuvered the sports car back onto the road and screeched off, satisfied at the completion of that job. A job where the end result was in flames at the bottom of a mountain.

Chapter One

"Girls on Film" by Duran Duran echoed across the Virginia Beach coastline. Glamour Girls Incorporated was doing their photo shoot for their summer catalog. The company had been searching for erotic Bahamas-like scenery without the Bahamas' price tag. Because of a plea from an old friend, they captured the very essence of the Bahamas in Derek Chase's back yard.

Derek Chase straightened his tie as he walked outside onto his wooden deck that overlooked the Atlantic Ocean. He draped the navy blue suit jacket over his arm and leaned against the frame of the patio entrance. He looked at the model that was surrounded by photography equipment. He had not seen her since he picked her up yesterday at the airport. Their opportunity to catch up on old times had fallen to the wayside. He smiled. She was spinning around and posing, smiling and laughing as if she had a little too much to drink on a lonely Friday night.

The caressing breeze of the beach took her white see-through scarf from her shoulders and loosely tossed it, and her naturally wavy, honey blonde hair, across her face throughout the series of poses. Her hazel eyes would flash a glance rivaling that of a tiger before the kill and her smile would comfort the soul as only an angel from heaven could do. She spun to face him and cocked her head toward the camera with a look of determination. Her backless, black bodysuit with the low cut front made a suggestion that could be boycotted by nuns and priests, while the diamond accessories that accompanied her ensemble could make the richest of burglars salivate. Her black jeans hugged her firm, yet feminine figure. It was almost pure anticipation that they would soon tear from her body. The camera was fighting to get as many pictures as possible. He looked on, focusing on specific movements and gestures of the enchantress in front of him.

She caught his stare and sent a look so seductive that his curiosity could only dare imagine the repercussions. He raised an eyebrow with a devilish smile that could only make her laugh into submission. She stopped spinning and waved at the photographer.

"Greg, that'll be all for now."

The photographer nodded and began to wind the film to his camera. She stepped out of the area that had been carefully mapped out for her display of animation. She walked over to him. Her movements proved that she was practicing for her strut along the catwalk, confident and determined.

"Are you trying to excite me?" Derek asked with a sheepish grin.

She smiled at his flirting and chose to engage it. "If I was trying to excite you, your pants would be to your ankles by now."

He rubbed his thin goatee and looked down at his navy blue suit pants. He smiled contemplating her remark. "Yes. I suppose they would."

She smiled shaking her head. "You're terrible. Don't you have a girlfriend?"

"Nope," He answered in what could be taken as a jubilant cheer. "My little black book has more lives than a litter of kittens."

"There must be someone out there," she asked.

"I'm sure there is." He responded with a sheepish grin. "Unfortunately, she doesn't know it yet."

"Derek Chase, you are a-"

"A kind, sweet-hearted gentleman," he interrupted. "Who is letting an old friend turn his house into a hotel full of beautiful women. Beautiful women who take pleasure in roaming around freely, wearing the skimpiest of clothing."

"Might I add that he is loving every minute of it?"

He smiled as Duran Duran was replaced by a dance version of "Amazing" by George Michael. She was right. He straightened his posture and outstretched his arms. "It's been a long time Courtney. I missed you."

She accepted his invitation for a hug. "I missed you too."

He sighed. He had missed her. His family history was never conducive to his personal life. He knew that his father's hopes of protecting his family required them to travel around the world for years. However, his father would occasionally need to return to the States to complete a few business transactions. Therefore to continue his children's education, he would continuously re-enroll them into the local high school until it was time to resume globe hopping. The arrangement his father set up with the various school boards were similar to that of parents who had children that were celebrities. It helped to dismiss any questions as to why they were always globe hopping. Derek did not become a United States resident until he was twenty-three.

Of course, it was during one of their brief stays in the States, when Courtney Lathaye and Derek Chase first met. It was in high school, and from the start, they hated each other. Their battlefield was in tenth grade homeroom, and their arsenals were the derogatory remarks and one liners most commonly associated with teenagers. It was a three-month war that made the Los Angeles Riots look like a day at Disneyland.

The weapon he used against Courtney's self-image, as well as her sanity, was not the jeer about the braces on her teeth or the insults about the zits on her face, but the crush she had on a red headed kid named Chip who also shared their homeroom. Chip had already known that Courtney had a crush on him. Therefore, Derek believed he could do no more harm than what was already done, when he made up nursery rhymes about Courtney and Chip.

For three months, his malicious teasing bombarded Courtney. Three months of absolute torture, until Derek met Tawanda Adams, a fifteen-year-old brainiac that could out-think some of her teachers. She had placed Derek as her object of desire, thus allowing Courtney to use the verbal weaponry against her tormentor. It took three weeks of verbal abuse from Courtney before a truce was formed. They had been friends ever since. Because Derek's father traveled around the globe, his enrollment in high school was sporadic at best. His longest enrollment period was four months when he played basketball. His friendship with Courtney served as an anchor to some type of normalcy of teenage livelihood. It kept him grounded.

"So how was Europe?" Derek asked pulling himself away from a long awaited hug.

"Busy." She responded. "You know how it is. Being glamorous is a twenty-four hour a day job."

"But you do it with such tenacity." He said with a smile. Despite the dorkiness she projected during their freshman year in high school, Courtney evolved. By her junior year her pimples on her face were replaced with unblemished color and the removal of her braces revealed a smile trying to outshine the sun. Like a caterpillar, she too had became a beautiful butterfly. It was no wonder many of the popular girls, that ignored her previously, saved face by electing her the captain of the varsity cheerleading squad.

Now when he looked at her, her maturity had blossomed again. Her slightly tanned faced seemed milky and her hazel eyes burned with energy. Her face was toned allowing her curves of her jaw to be perfectly rounded without losing the slight indentations of her dimples when she smiled. Her arched eyebrows were professionally groomed allowing her nose to sit comfortably on her face. Her body also had the right blend of attributes. As he noticed before, her figure was a sculpted masterpiece. Unlike her underweight modeling colleagues, he could hug her without snapping her in half. Courtney's shape complimented her profession. From the pictures he saw in the magazines she autographed for him, her body flaunted its flawlessness and deceptively enticed men without them even knowing that they were addicted to her beauty. She was truly a work of art and he imagined that someone in Heaven was still patting themselves on the back for job well done. It was easy to understand why she was on the cover of so many magazines around the world.

She smiled. "Comes with the trade." She responded grabbing Derek's arm and leading him into the beach house. "How's the P.I. business?"

"Not too bad. I'm pretty much on a work as they come kinda schedule."

Courtney scanned the beach house and the scenery. "You don't seem to be doing too shabby."

"Sweetheart, I'm the best."

"That's what they all say."

"I wasn't talking about the P.I. stuff. I gotta second job."

"Oh yeah," Courtney taunted. "As what?"

The black detective watched her eyes take their turn at grading his appearance. He too had changed a lot from high school. His face had finally made the compromise of boyish looks with adult maturity. His dark caramel complexion enhanced the color of his brown eyes and the creaminess of his face. The hair on his head was trimmed neatly, as well as the goatee that surrounded the contours of his mouth. His daily martial arts Kata along with his rigorous workout three times a week strengthened his 215-pound body and buffed his six-foot figure. At first glance, people generally thought he was a running back for some nearby football team and even though the thought never crossed his mind, he imagined he too could showcase his own qualities within the pages of a calendar or on the cover of a magazine.

He chuckled innocently, "You'd have to pay me to find out."

Courtney shoved him in the shoulder with a smile as she glanced around the beach house. The large bay window over-looking the beach and the Atlantic Ocean was breath taking. The beige sectional sofa, separating the living room with a fireplace from the rest of the dwelling, invited Courtney to enjoy a more relaxed part of the beach house. However, despite her deepest desires to snuggle deep within the soft plush pillows of the sofa, she still had a schedule to maintain. Glamour Girls Incorporated had a week before they started their fall catalog photo shoot in New York.

She placed her arm around his waist and turned towards the photographer. "Greg, will you take our picture?"

The photographer gave a big smile as he picked up another camera. "Sure thing Ms. Lathaye."

"You can play now," she said as her photographer took aim with the camera. "But wait. The day will come when the old dog will need to dig up some bones and get a six-bedroom dog house."

They both smiled as he snapped a couple of shots. He gave a "thumbs up". "I'll have these developed this afternoon Ms. Lathaye."

She nodded with a smile of approval as the photographer went back to checking his equipment. The warm summer breeze coming from the ocean waved her hair into her face as she turned to face him.

"You know Courtney," Derek began as she moved the strands of her honey blonde hair from her cheek. He grabbed the hands of the model and cupped them with his. The diamond charm bracelet hung loosely as Courtney looked into his hazel eyes. "You were never a bone that was buried."

"Oh no you don't," she retreated. "We're not going to get into this conversation again."

"But Courtney," he said as she pulled her hands out of his hands.

"Derek," she started. "I know you love me and I love you too. You mean more to me than anything in this world. I would do anything for you, but don't ask me to do this. Don't ask me to be somebody I can't. Not now. Not at this point of my life. It's unfair to you and to me."

He lowered his head in submission. He was in love with Courtney from the first day they met. It took two semesters and a lot of flowers, but he was finally able to win her heart. They dated throughout their senior year. He was prepared to marry her, but refused to let her dreams die. She wanted to be an actress and go to Hollywood. He loved her so much that he did not have the courage to deny her. So, he shuffled his feelings into a corner of his heart and kept them hidden from her. That method worked until he watched her get off the plane. Despite his ill-timed experiences involving those he loved and his vow of keeping passion at bay, he could not deny his love for her. It would not be long before his denial would inspire tragic consequences, thus he still needed to keep his feelings for her a secret.

"I know Courtney. You're right." He opened his arms and hugged her. "I'm sorry."

Courtney smiled as she hugged him back, squeezing harder than her previous hug. He knew that when it came to him, she had mixed feelings, and that her best way to deal with those feelings was to dismiss and ignore them. It worked when she was on the other side of the planet, but could her mixed feelings be back?

"Well, don't let it happen again."

"Mr. Chase?" came a soft voice from behind. He turned to find a tall woman with brown, wavy hair walking up. He recognized her as Olivia Lockehart, the on-location manager for Glamour Girls Incorporated. Courtney had described her as a forty plus year old woman with a stone cold attitude.

When he met Ms. Lockehart for the first time at the airport, he was taken aback by her young appearance. When she stepped out of the private jet, her long brown hair stiffened in the Virginian breeze. She wore little makeup. Her slender face accented the curves of her chin without bringing notice to her ears. Courtney had mentioned that they sometimes managed to emerge from her head like radar dishes attempting to hear audience feedback. Today, they seemed pinned underneath the smooth mane of brown hair. She had full lips that look as soft as a pillow filled with feathers. She also seemed to be very physically fit. He stared in awe at her long and muscular legs as she walked down the small staircase of the aircraft. Her red business suit with black trim suggested an authority rivaling that of an army general. Her strong handshake and fiery green eyes confirmed her authority, as well as the attitude Courtney warned about.

However, he had hardly seen Olivia Lockehart at the beach house. She seemed to be running errands for the models or setting up the different locations for the many photo shoots they had to complete in Virginia Beach before their trip to New York. If there was a stone cold attitude, Derek had not seen it.

"I just wanted to extend my gratitude, for the use of your beach house. You have saved my company thousands of dollars."

He smiled. "Just doing my duty for God and country."

Olivia Lockehart smiled. Her seductiveness was beginning to seep through her stone cold facade. "You were right Courtney, he is a charmer." She grabbed his hand and shook it. "Thank you again Mr. Chase," and with that, she walked off towards a corner of the deck where a group of models were huddled together.

He glanced at Courtney. "A charmer, huh?"

She wrapped her arms around his waist and smiled. "And a cute one too," she replied and she kissed him on the cheek.

Derek took a glance at his watch and was quickly reminded of the time. He had an engagement that he would be late for if he decided to spend another moment with his houseguest. "I'm sorry Courtney, I gotta go."

"What? You have a hot date or somethin'?" She asked defensively.

He kissed her on the forehead. "As a matter of fact. I promised somebody brunch."

"Is she cute?"

Derek too a step backwards with a raised eyebrow and a charming smile. "She's model material."

"She better be." Courtney remarked. "I wouldn't want you to lower your standards."

Derek chuckled. "Make me an honest man so I'll never have to."

She shook her head. "Nah. This is too much fun."

He decided not to pursue the issue any further. "I need to go. I'll be back soon," he said as he started heading for the front door. He soon bumped into another model. She was a thin brunette, wearing a bikini. He mouthed sorry as he tried to get out of her way. "Oh, and Courtney?" He began as he opened the front door. He looked at her with a devilish smile.

"Yeah?"

"Be good."

"I can't promise you that." She said. She blew a kiss as he raised his hand good-bye.

He stepped out of the front door of his beach house leaving one mystery, for another. Seeing Courtney was bringing up many old feelings, fantasies and doubts. Was he ready to settle down?

He dismissed the thoughts from his mind. With Courtney doing the photo shoot in his back yard, he would have ample time to gather and decipher those feelings soon enough. Now, it was time to fulfill a promise and investigate another relationship. A

relationship that was formed on the brink of chaos and disorder.

<u>**Chapter Two**</u>:

The cafeteria of Virginia Beach General Hospital seemed small in comparison to the staff that resided there. Throughout brunch, his mind was asking how it could accommodate the bevy of doctors, nurses, and staff, in addition to the many patients and their family members. But, that was not important. What was important, was the attractive doctor across from him. The short sleeved blue hospital shirt did very little to hide her toned arms. He knew that she took pride in her health and the rest of her physique complimented her athletic appetite. There were traces of blonde strands peeking through her dark brown hair that was corralled into a ponytail. Her light mocha skin accented her brown eyes and perfectly arched eyebrows. His idea of her being model material was dead on. This was the third time they had the opportunity to have brunch together. They used their time at brunch to learn more about each other. She intrigued him. She was as smart as she was beautiful. However, despite her beauty, his mind was still drifting away from the woman in front of him and focusing on Courtney. He could hear his brunch companion talking to him, but her words were not registering.

Dr. Shannon Gellar took a sip of her juice before continuing. "You didn't hear a word I said, did you?"

His ears perked up and he straightened his posture. "Wha-? Of course I heard what you said."

Dr. Gellar giggled. "Sure. So you agree about what I said about us seeing other people?"

Derek smiled. "Most definitely. See other people."

Dr. Gellar shook her head. "Derek, you weren't listening to me. We're not even dating. I was talking about that armored car heist in Paris. Over ten million dollars in African diamonds were stolen."

"Ten million dollars?"

Dr. Gellar nodded. "Yeah. It's all over CNN. But you would know that if you had been paying attention to me."

"I'm sorry Doc."

"What's up Derek?" Dr. Gellar asked. "You've been distracted throughout brunch." She took another sip of her drink before continuing. "What's her name?"

He smiled defensively. "What makes you think it's a woman?"

She took in a spoonful of yogurt before answering. "Call it Doctor-Patient privilege. I've only known you for about a month, and very rarely are you distracted. Not to mention, you flirt with me every chance you get. You practically had to kill yourself to get me to go to brunch a third time, which you've been quiet throughout.

So, my thought is there's a woman involved and I'd like to know the name of the girl that has the infallible Derek Chase tongue-tied and twisted."

He gave a humpf and a smile. "Damn Doc," he replied. "I think I liked it better when I thought we were dating. Maybe I'll just tune out again."

"Derek!"

He chuckled playfully. "Her name is Courtney."

"Courtney? She must be heaven sent in order for you to be this pre-occupied."

"Sometimes, I think she is."

"Just sometimes?"

Derek cocked his head slightly before answering. "I don't know Doc. It's weird. I have loved this woman from the first day I met her. Even with me traveling around the world with my family, I had a chance to date her in high school. Happiest year of my life. We loved each other so much. By the time graduation came around, I was set to marry her. I even bought the ring and was going to propose after we received our diplomas."

Dr. Gellar smiled. "Wow. How sweet. I didn't think there was a woman out there that could tie you down."

"Well, if there is one, it's Courtney."

Dr. Gellar swallowed another sip of her juice. "So what happened?"

He shrugged and sighed. "I let her get away."

"Huh?" she responded. Her face seemed dazed as she processed the information. "Why?"

"Courtney always wanted to go Hollywood and be a big time movie actress. The week before graduation, she was contacted by a modeling agency in Los Angeles. I knew that she loved me so much that if I proposed, she would marry me and stay here. I didn't have the heart to deny her from her dreams. So I buried the ring under the beach house, graduated, helped her pack, watched her board the plane and fly away."

"And now she's back and those feelings have returned."

Derek nodded. "Except this time, it's different. Part of me wants to do everything I can to win her back, but the other part is keeping her at a distance. Funny thing is, I think she's going through the same thing."

"Let me guess." She began. "That whole theory about 'I can't love someone because sooner or later they'll wind up dead.'"

Derek shook his head. He knew that she was referring to his past relationships. His relationship with his mother was ripped away from him at an early age when she was killed in a car accident. It left him yearning for maternal affection. The young relationship with his boss Tessa Taylor was ended prematurely by her business partner. Therefore, he never had the opportunity to repay her for giving him a second chance to rebuild his life from the stigma of being an outcast from the Virginia Beach Police department. In addition, he almost forfeited the relationship he had with Elizabeth Marie Companstella. She was the only person from the Virginia Beach Police department who stood by his side throughout his departure from his duty to serve and protect. Their one night of raw passion had them following a course of continued intimacy between two friends. However, that came to a sudden halt when she was shot in the line of duty attending to his needs. It was then that he made a vow to keep pure love at bay. It was a vow that Courtney's return was threatening to violate, and a vow that Dr. Gellar was desperately trying to dismiss.

"It's not that simple." He concluded.

Her brown eyes glared at him. "Yes it is. If you love her, let her know that you love her and stop beating around the bush. Think of it this way; if you let her get away this time, you'll never have the opportunity to tell her how you feel and you'll go through the rest of your life wondering what could've been."

Derek's pager chimed before he could respond. He glanced down and raised his eyebrows; somewhat relieved that Dr. Gellar's psychotherapy was coming to a close. He knew she was right, but denied himself from acting upon her suggestions. If he gave in to his desire, he would lose her, but the feelings he had for her were almost too much to contain. For now, his vow still continued the fight.

"I'm sorry Doc," he said looking back at her. She was shaking her head as she took one final sip of her juice. "I'm being summoned. We'll have to continue this conversation some other time." He feigned.

She must have known his sincerity was a farce. "Sure. Whenever you're ready. Just promise me that you'll think about this. True love only comes around twice in a lifetime. After that, there is no third strike. There is no do-over. Just wishing."

Derek stood up, leaned across the table and kissed her on the cheek. "I'll think about it. Thank you for brunch."

She smiled as he began his departure. "You're welcome. Stop being so damn

stubborn and remember what I said."

He nodded as she watched him leave the cozy hospital cafeteria. She hoped that

despite Derek's stubbornness, which was born from circumstances beyond his control,

the destiny that true love had in store for him would ultimately be carried out. She

gave a humpf as she anticipated their next conversation.

<u>**Chapter Three**</u>:

"Good morning." Derek said as he opened the door to Sydney Taylor's office. "Your page just saved me from another session of psycho-analytical babblecock. I tell you-" He stopped abruptly when he looked over at Sydney's desk to find that there was a well-dressed couple standing in front of it. He unintentionally had interrupted a meeting. "I'm sorry." He began. "I didn't know you were in a meeting. Sandra wasn't at her desk and–"

"It's okay." Said the gentleman. His black suit was crisp and neat. His sandy brown hair looked like it was recently trimmed. He was a built broad-shouldered man who looked like he loved to play sports. The smile on his face was genuine. "We were just finishing."

"Forgive the interruption," Sydney interjected. "Mr. And Mrs. Leiding, I'd like you to meet Derek Chase. He is the private investigator for Garrett and Taylor."

Mr. Leiding took a step towards Derek and extended his hand. "Please call me Jon, and this is my wife Christine."

"Pleased to meet you." Derek said as he shook Jon Leiding's hand. It was a firm handshake, one that projected professionalism as well as pleasantries. "Again, I'm sorry to interrupt."

Jon's wife, Christine was professionally dressed in a black pants suit ensemble. She had long strawberry blonde hair that complimented her slightly tanned face. She too took a step towards Derek extending her hand. When he shook it, her grip was firm like her husband's and her smile was just as genuine. She quickly dismissed his apology. "No, don't apologize. You came in at the right time." She said just before she turned and picked up her leather bound planner from Sydney's mahogany desk.

"The Leidings own the nationally acclaimed website, The Party Kitchen." Sydney began as she stepped away from her desk. "As of today, their business is international. We'll be representing them through this new and exciting phase."

"Who would've thought that two years ago we were just starting out?" said Jon. "It's amazing. But I can't take the credit. That all belongs to this lovely lady here."

His wife smiled in attempt to hide her blushing modesty. "Don't listen to him, we both worked hard at this."

Derek smiled. It was nice to see hard working people accomplish their dreams and their goals. His next statement sounded like he was the corporate spokesman in a commercial. "Well, you are in good hands. Garrett and Taylor thrives on going the distance for its clientele."

Sydney smiled as she began to lead them out of her office. "I will have the necessary paperwork filed by end of business today."

"Again, thank you for your help." Christine said. "I'm extremely pleased at how amiable this entire process was."

Sydney continued smiling as she extended her hand. "It's my job to keep it that way. Thank you for your time. I will be in touch."

They both smiled courteously as they shook her hand and said thank you. Sydney watched them walk through the reception area and exit through the heavy glass doors of Garrett and Taylor Law. She then turned and focused on Derek.

"I'm sorry for interrupting." He apologized.

Sydney chuckled as she started for her desk. "Don't worry about it. The meeting was done about ten minutes before you came in. We were just talking about how quickly a person's life can change. Did you know that before The Party Kitchen became successful, Christine was a project manager for a finance company and Jon was a DJ? It hasn't been that long ago that I was a lawyer for the United States Navy. Look at me now. I'm in charge of a multi-million dollar law firm." She took a seat and sighed. "You never know what life has waiting for you around the corner."

Derek nodded as he took a seat. Sydney Taylor was a very attractive woman. Her hair was long and black allowing her to project a very business-like appearance. She wore make-up that accented her proportionately adequate, tanned face and blue eyes. Her skin was not as smooth as the Glamour Girl models staying at his house, but it was soft to the touch and look as if it was being preserved with the utmost care. She was a voluptuous woman with Navy-groomed muscle tone, but made sure that her attire did little to bring attention to it.

He smiled at his employer. "No, but that's why you surround yourself with people you love and trust. So when you go around that corner, they'll be there to share in your triumphs and your defeats."

"You sound like a man of experience."

Derek smiled as he allowed himself to sink in the leather chair. "Probably more than I'll ever let on." He then sat up as he changed the subject. "You paged me?"

"Yes." Sydney answered as she sat up. "Have you ever been employed as a bodyguard?" She asked. The successor to Garrett and Taylor Law crossed her legs as she took the file on her desk and placed it in her desk drawer. Her sister helped to build the corporate law firm from the ground up and made it her duty to establish its impeccable reputation. She gave her life fulfilling that mission. Despite Tessa Taylor's tragic death at the hands of her business partner Kevin Garrett, a little over a month ago, Sydney seemed to be adjusting fine with the new responsibilities.

"No," Derek answered. "I can't say that I have."

"Do you have an issue with being one?"

"No. I think I can handle it."

"Good," she replied standing up from the mahogany desk. "Because I have your assignment." She stepped over to the file cabinet. The matching mahogany bookshelves hid the metallic storage units from view. She opened it and quickly withdrew a manila envelope. She closed the drawer and smiled with satisfaction as she handed the file to him.

"His name is Walter Mallott." She began as she returned to her leather chair. "He is an accountant for Jupiter Hardware on Holland Road here in Virginia Beach. The U.S. Attorney's office is using his testimony to convict the owner Tony Cooke, of money laundering. The trial will take place in Virginia Beach and the U.S. District Attorney's office has asked for our assistance. Because we specialize in corporate law, I will be the co-prosecutor. Now, here's where you come in. Mr. Mallott is convinced that Mr. Cooke is trying to have him killed and the United States government doesn't want to take any chances. All you'll be doing is baby-sitting for a couple of days until the U.S. marshals come in. It's a walk in the park."

The detective scanned the papers inside the file and found Mr. Mallott's address and his picture. He guessed that Mallott was somewhere in his forties. His face was haggard and sported a few wrinkles. His cheeks were puffy with red splotches matching the abundance of curly red hair on top of his face. He looked as if the fight had been drained from his body. He was certainly recognizable possibly making it a challenge to protect him. However, he could move Mr. Mallott to his beach house in which case he could keep his eye on him while entertaining Courtney and the ladies of Glamour Girls Inc. Besides, his father had the house wired with a state of the art security system. Though he knew nothing in his line of work was a walk in the park, this would be as close as it would come.

"I'll move him to -

Sydney quickly interrupted with a brisk wave of the hand. "Only you will be privy to where he is. Sometimes it's best that I don't know these things."

"Okay," Derek responded. "Mr. Mallott will temporarily disappear." He closed the file and placed it back on her desk. He smiled at her as he asked his next question. "So how are you doing? Emotionally?"

She smiled back while reflecting on his question. She picked up the picture of her and her sister when they were in college. He could see her bringing those memories back to life forcing him to remember the woman who gave him a second chance.

Tessa Taylor was able to make a business suit seductive as well as powerful. The blonde attorney, like her sister, was a young, very attractive, voluptuous woman. However, she wore little make-up because she was aware of her natural beauty. Her velvety peach colored face was always fresh with energy and her dark green eyes incessantly flashed with intensity. He remembered that she wore sweet perfume that invigorating to the senses. He remembered how he wished he had more time with her realizing that Sydney must have been yearned for the same thing.

She gave a long sigh. "It's hard at times. Military cases are different from Business Law. She's not here to offer any advice or guide me in the right direction. Not to mention that I've looked over every single case file that's pending and Garrett and Taylor is up to its eyeballs in lawsuits. Honestly, I'm feeling a bit overwhelmed." She sighed as she made her next statement. "I miss her Derek."

"I miss her too." He admitted remembering his brief encounter with Tessa Taylor.

Tessa Taylor paused and then closed the dossier. She then sat back in her chair and he watched her demeanor become more professional. "Mr. Chase, let me get straight to the point. I'm not sure if you are the right person for this job. I mean, you were an honor roll student at Ithaca and dropped out a semester before graduating with a masters in criminal justice. You were also a police officer for the City of Virginia Beach, and we both know what happened with that. Honestly, your history says that you seem like a competent person who can get the job done. However, there have been too many unfortunate incidents, which detour you from your goal. And I don't see you hurrying back to get on the right path. To sum it up for you Mr. Chase, at Garrett and Taylor, we expect you to go the distance giving two hundred percent of yourself all the way, despite the obstacles. Tell me; can you bring that quality to Garrett and Taylor? Please, make an impression on me Mr. Chase."

He took a minute and sat back in the leather chair. He was coming to the conclusion that this interview would soon have the same results as all the others. No company wanted to hire a graduate school dropout and an ex-cop with a less than perfect background.

He looked at the blonde interviewer before him and quickly studied her body. His eyes searched. She was more attractive than when he first met her a year ago. She was a young, very attractive, voluptuous woman that wore little make-up, because she was aware of her natural beauty. Her peach colored face was fresh with energy and her dark green eyes flashed with intensity. Her perfume was sweet as she sat across from him. Her navy blue business suit was powerful, yet it defined her seductiveness. It was no wonder she was the most sought after attorney in Virginia. Her beauty complimented the long list of degrees and awards that decorated her office. He decided that if he were not going to get the job, he would definitely make an impression. He crossed his legs, folded his arms, and smiled. He had the perfect response. "You're either wearing a thong or no panties at all."

"I beg your pardon?"

He continued with his observation. "You're a very bright and intelligent individual as suggested from the neatly framed degrees on the walls. The picture of your family tells me that they are upper middle class, yet you yourself have very expensive taste since you have a mahogany desk and soft leather chairs in your office. I would guess that you like the beach, since your office overlooks the Atlantic and with the small amount of plants, I would say that you like to be outdoors."

"What does all that have to do with me wearing or not wearing underwear?"

The investigator chuckled. "Nothing at all. I watched you when you escorted me into your office. There were no panty lines in your skirt, but if I had to choose, I would say that you were wearing a thong. You don't look like the type that would go without underwear. But then again, I could be wrong."

Tessa smiled. "Excuse me Mr. Chase, but this could be considered as sexual harassment. I could make sure that you never work in this state again."

"I understand that, but I made an impression. That is what you asked for. Is it not?"

Tessa smiled as she scribbled a note in file. "Mr. Chase, I'm going to do something that I hope you don't make me regret later. I'm going to take a chance on you. I expect you to be here Monday morning at 8 AM sharp. We have to get you familiar with the security set-up and fill out the paperwork for payroll," She then stood up and extended her hand. Derek stood and accepted the handshake. "Welcome to Garrett and Taylor."

He was still in shock when he said. "Thank you Ms. Taylor."

"Please, call me Tessa, and just to clear the air. You were right about a lot of things. I like to be outdoors. My family lives on the outskirts of Boston in a community that is considered upper middle class, and I am very proud of my accomplishments."

"What about the underwear theory?" He dared to ask.

Tessa folded her arms and smiled devilishly. "Well, Mr. Chase, I guess that is one mystery you'll have a hard time solving."

From the doorway, he watched the police department's forensics team taking snapshots of the scenery trying to piece together various clues. *It looked like it was going to be a tough assignment. The apartment had been torn apart. It was as if a tornado had been born in the middle of the living room and unmercifully displayed its insatiable appetite for destruction. The burgundy couch and love seat had been ripped open like gutted fish. The glass coffee table separating them, were now many little islands of glass splinters. Looking past the living room through the breakfast bar, he could see the refrigerator door and the kitchen cabinets had been thrown open and their contents exhibited across the counters. He suspected much of the same throughout the apartment. There was an oak desk in the far corner by the kitchen. It had been toppled over, its desk drawers strewn across the floor with their contents* emptied on the carpet. The awards and framed pictures that were once on the wall above the desk, sat on the floor-cracked open. A computer monitor with a busted screen had somehow managed to travel to the other side of the room where it positioned itself next to a plant that had been uprooted and discarded. At the far wall leading to the bedrooms were the remnants of an aquarium. It had been emptied out onto the carpet, soaking it with a variety of fish and aquarium toys that the detectives were still having a hard time avoiding. In the center of that mishap was a large black bag as the sum of one's ill-timed actions and a sad reminder of how precious life was.

The night air seemed chilly for a summer night as Derek and Lt. Austin stepped out onto the observation deck of Lynnhaven One. They found Kevin and Sydney standing across from one another with the lights of the Chesapeake Bay Bridge serving as a lighted backdrop. However, the detective's attention was not focused on the nightlights, but the trembling hand of Kevin Garrett. The lawyer was holding Tessa's Walther PPK and had it aimed at Sydney. Austin had immediately withdrew his weapon and pointed it towards the armed attorney.

"Drop the gun Mr. Garrett!"

Kevin looked at the two intruders and then back at Sydney who was backing away from him. His hands trembled even more. "She doesn't understand."

"Drop the gun now!" Austin ordered.

"Can't you see what she's doing to me?"

Derek placed a hand on Austin's shoulder as he took a step forward. "Kevin? What is she doing to you?"

He could see a tear roll down the cheek of the hostage taker. "She wouldn't listen to me! She's gonna ruin everything! Heather wouldn't understand!" He pointed towards Sydney. "She and I spent every waking moment together. I loved her! When she told me she was pregnant, I didn't know how to handle it. I went bezerk! I went over to her house to look for her medical records and she came home early. We got into an argument and I.....I hit her. She got scared and pulled out her gun."

"And you shot her?"

"It was an accident!" and Kevin broke down in tears.

"I know it was an accident and I know you loved Tessa."

"But....Heather?"

"You still love her don't you?"

Kevin nodded as a few more tears rolled down his face.

"And she loves you?"

The attorney nodded again and shook the gun at Sydney. "But I can't let her ruin everything! I just can't! You hear that Tessa? I won't let you ruin everything you selfish bitch!"

Derek drew closer realizing that Sydney's resemblance to her sister had Kevin walking a fine line between past and present. It was become an increasingly volatile situation. He took another step closer to the gun-toting attorney. He could almost reach out and take the gun. "Look at me." Derek said calmly. Kevin turned his head as the gun shook wildly. "It's over Kevin. Tessa can't hurt you anymore."

"She can't? But-

"It's over." The private investigator said softly as he reached up and lowered the gun in Kevin's shaking hand. In one quick movement, he reverted back to his police training and put Kevin in an arm lock and forced him to the ground. Austin ran up re-holstering his weapon and unveiling a pair of handcuffs as Derek slowly pried Kevin's fingers away from the gun that killed his business partner.

He looked over at Sydney who was beginning to shake like a leaf. Austin knelt down and snapped the metallic bracelets on Kevin's wrist and began reading him his Miranda Rights. "Kevin Garrett, you are under arrest for the murder of Tessa Taylor. You have the right to remain silent."

Derek stood as Sydney ran up to him. Tears were welling up in her face as she wrapped her arms around him. He did his best to comfort her. "I still can't believe he killed Tessa," she cried. "When he told me-

"Shh..." he comforted. "It's gonna be okay. It's all over now."

He looked over at Kevin who was still having his rights read to him as Austin hoisted him to his feet. His tears had stopped, but his face was still glazed over. The police Lt. yanked him forward and began towards the door exiting the observation deck.

"No!" Kevin yelled as he resisted. "You can't!" and he snatched himself away from Austin's grip and ran away from him.

"Goddamn it!" Austin said mainly to himself as he took chase. "Come back here!"

Derek and Sydney watched as Kevin ran full sprint towards the ledge of the observation deck with Austin quick on his heels. They stared in horror as Kevin dove head-first over the railing. Austin reached out for him, but the expression on his face confirmed his failure. The Lt. lowered his head in pity.

Derek quickly returned from the past when Sydney asked. "Are you alright?"

"Sure." Derek answered realizing that he had been staring over Sydney's shoulder and out the window. "Just thinking about everything that happened."

"Yeah, I haven't been able to get it out of my head either." Sydney straightened her jacket as she sat up in her chair. The telephone on her desk beeped. Saundra must have returned from her errand. "Well, there's nothing I can do about it now." She pressed a button on her phone to accept the incoming transmission. "Yes, Saundra?"

"Mr. Collings is here to see you."

"I'll be there in a moment. Thank you Saundra."

Derek raised his eyebrows as he stood up. "Mr. Collings? Why does that name sound familiar?"

Sydney smiled. "It should sound familiar. Ever heard of Sage Linens."

"Who hasn't?" He then raised an eyebrow realizing what was transpiring.. "You have an appointment with Sage Collings? As in Sage Collings, the Beverly Hills manufacturer of fine linens?"

"The one and the same." Sydney said as she nodded again. "He's opening a call-center and a warehouse in Virginia Beach and asked us to draw up the legal paperwork."

"Garrett and Taylor goes Hollywood." Derek smiled. "Saundra must be going crazy out there. Probably trying to get the guy's autograph now."

Sydney made an effort to hide her giggle. "She's already asked to see if I can get an employee discount."

"An employee discount?" He chuckled with a sigh. "What will she think of next?"

Sydney nodded as she agreed. "I shudder the thought." She then sighed. "Though, I don't know what I would have done without her. She's been a big help in getting things back to normal around here."

Derek smiled as Sydney stood up from her chair. Saundra Wilkins was finishing up her junior year at Virginia Wesleyan, one of the local colleges, as a summer intern for Garrett and Taylor. She suffered through Tessa's passing along with him and Sydney, and proved to be very useful throughout his investigation. Sydney's gratitude for the college student was not only business related, but a personal one as well.

"Well," Derek began. "An employee discount may not be a bad idea. I could use some Egyptian cotton bed sheets."

She smirked. "I will not ask him for an employee discount. Besides, what do you need with Egypt-" and she caught the devilish smile spreading across his face. "On second thought, I'd rather not know."

He laughed as he started for the door. " I do have a life outside of this office."

She laughed with him. "Please spare me the sordid details and go get to work."

<u>**Chapter Four**</u>:

The black Ferrari 355 rolled slowly to a standstill on the concrete driveway of the Ramada Plaza Resort Oceanfront. He pulled in behind a cream colored Jaguar as he watched the valet hurry from his wooden post at the front entrance towards the Italian import.

He opened the door as he turned the ignition off. He stepped out of his car and quickly looked over at the valet with a smile. "I'm just here to pick someone up. Shouldn't be more than five minutes."

The valet stopped and nodded. Derek could tell that the valet was a little disappointed that there would be no tip from the Ferrari owner. He closed the door to the sports car and walked across the driveway towards the glass designer doors of the Ramada. One of the valets opened the door sharing the same expression as the valet that greeted him. He nodded with a thank you and walked inside the ocean resort hotel.

His nose immediately picked up the fresh scent of the carpet deodorizer mixed in with the bitter salty air coming from the ocean. He looked around the front lobby taking in his surroundings.

The first thing he noticed was the opposite side of the hotel. He had a panoramic view of the Atlantic Ocean. In the middle of this view were two glass doors with the Ramada logo. They were propped open, gesturing for all to roam freely between the hotel, "The Boardwalk" of Atlantic Avenue with its specialty shops, and the beach. A stiff breeze rustled the lapel of his jacket as he listened to the soft relaxing noise of the ocean. With the exception of that and the soft music playing in the background, all was quiet in the front lobby.

His head turned towards the front desk. It was a dark, multicolored marble with a heavy gloss. There were two guest check-in attendants. One attendant wore glasses and had short red hair. She was on the telephone negotiating prices with a prospective guest. The other attendant seemed uncomfortable in the maroon colored vest and tuxedo shirt. He was checking in an older couple that Derek believed were the owners of the cream Jaguar out front. A comical thought entered his mind. He wondered if the valet, that attempted to park his car received the same response when he tried to park their Jaguar. Well, some people were more protective over their vehicles than others.

He straightened the lapel of his jacket as he began his way over to the front desk. He stepped in front of the woman that was conversing on the telephone. She smiled to acknowledge his presence. She nodded her head a few times before taking a pen and writing down some information. She then thanked the person for calling as she jotted down some notes and then quickly diverted her attention towards him.

"Thank you for choosing the Ramada Plaza Resort Oceanfront," she began. "We are the premiere five-star resort hotel with the award winning Gus's Mariner Restaurant. With being the largest hotel on the oceanfront, we are fully equipped with smoking and non-smoking rooms for your convenience and offer a state-of-the-art indoor recreational center for those who like to work out. On the other hand, for those who rather just sit down and relax, we also offer an energy efficient spa with aromatherapy. Some of our other features include twenty-four hour room service and cable television with HBO and Showtime at no cost to you. Here at the Ramada, we go out of our way to make your stay as pleasant as possible."

He raised an eyebrow as he complimented her ability to make a rehearsed speech sound genuinely pleasant. "My name is Melissa, will you be checking in today sir?"

He smiled as he shook his head. "No. I'm actually here to pick up someone. Can you tell me which room, a Mr. Walter Mallott is staying in?"

"Normally, we do not give out our guests' room numbers." She smiled as she looked down at the computer terminal. "But, he seems to be one of our more popular guests today," she said as her fingers started dancing over the keyboard. "This morning, he was visited by a woman he tried passing off as his sister," she chuckled. "If she was his sister, then I'm the long lost daughter of Brad Pitt. This woman looked like the type who only works the night shift, if you get my drift. She had a crap load of make-up on. She left about a half hour ago."

"Has there been anybody else looking for him?"

"Funny you should ask that. There were these two guys, maybe about ten minutes before you that were looking for him. Big guys. Looked like they played hockey or something. They called up to his room, but there was no answer. They went looking around the hotel for him."

Derek raised an eyebrow wondering if those two men were sent by Mallott's boss. He figured he would have to get to Mallott before they did or face the consequence of failing to complete his assignment.

"The room is still being paid for by Garrett and Taylor Law Firm correct?"

He could see the computer screen flicker across the woman's eyeglasses. She nodded. "Yes it is."

"Could you please start the check-out procedures for Mr. Mallott and send the bill to Garrett and Taylor Law?"

She looked at her screen, somewhat confused at the request. She looked up at him and caught the request from his hazel brown eyes. She surrendered with a smile. "Sure. I'll start the paperwork at once. It'll be ready for you to sign when you get back."

"Thank you," he replied. "Which way to the hotel bar?"

She pointed at the glass sliding doors leading out towards the boardwalk and the beach. "Go through the glass doors and take a left. It's by the pool. You can't miss it."

"You've been a big help. Thanks again," and with that he started off towards the glass doors.

He was hoping that if Walter Mallott knew that two men, who looked like hockey players, were looking for him, he would go to the most crowded place in the hotel. The hotel bar would be crowded enough to avoid a scene and make a quick exit if necessary.

With the glass doors open, a rush of salty ocean airbrushed past him as he stepped onto the patio. He scanned the hotel setting for his quarry. Directly in front he could see the waves splashing against the sand. Three children were nearby building a sandcastle as their parents sat in close proximity. Beyond them skimming across the water were a pair of windsurfers. He looked up as he heard the engine of a prop plane. In continuing with its summertime duties, the red, single engine prop plane flew proudly dragging the long banner advertising the "all-you-could-eat" buffet at one of the local restaurants on Atlantic Avenue. It was a beautiful day to be a tourist in Virginia Beach.

He then scanned the bar by the pool. Two tanned women, in bikinis had swam up and emerged from the hotel's Olympic size pool. They stepped up towards the bar conversing with each other. One had dark black hair and the other was a red head. They used their fingers to strain the pool water from their glamorous manes. He could not help but notice the droplets of water dripping from their shapely bodies. He was tempted to buy them both a drink when he noticed that someone else was admiring them as well.

Derek shook his head as Walter Mallott appeared from the other side of the bar. He was wearing khaki shorts and maroon polo shirt. In his hand he carried a coconut with a straw. He looked exactly like his picture. He was slightly obese and his face

housed an intricate road map of wrinkles. His curly red hair and tanned face made him

look like a life sized Howdy Doody doll on vacation or a successful used car salesman

from Toronto. As the detective's quarry positioned himself between the two women, it

was evident that Walter Mallott was about to act upon Derek's idea.

The detective's attention diverted when he saw two men stepping out of the glass

doors on the other side of the patio. They were indeed two big, handsomely dressed

men. He guessed they were the two hockey players the front desk clerk had mentioned

earlier. It was time for Walter Mallott to check out of his fantasy, before he found

himself checking into Virginia Beach General Hospital.

Giving an occasional glance at the two men, who were now scouring the pool

area, Derek stepped up behind Walter. He almost released a guffaw when he heard

Walter tell the two women that he was a government spy on vacation from assignment

in Paris. He snapped Walter out of his fantasy by placing his hand on the con man's

shoulder. He could feel the body of the sales manager stiffening.

"Mr. Mallott," the detective began. "I'm from Garrett and Taylor Law. I would

like to direct your attention to the two large men surveying the pool area." Mallott

turned. "Do you see them?"

Mallott looked around and nodded when he saw the two hulking figures.

"They are here to make sure that you never get a chance to testify against your

former employer. My job is to make sure that they never get the chance to get to you.

So, I ask that you do everything I tell you from this point on. That sounds like a

reasonable request, doesn't it?"

Again Mallott nodded.

The detective watched the two men and he began to move Walter away from the

bar that had served as his hiding place. It would only be a matter of time before they

were found.

"You ladies have a good day," Walter said blowing kisses as Derek dragged him

along. He watched Mallott salivate over what could have been and suddenly saw his

body jerk sideways. Mallott had ran into a hotel waiter with a tray full of drinks. He

watched helplessly as the hotel waiter fell into the hotel swimming pool.

The commotion coupled with the loud splash caught the attention of the two

henchmen. They quickly discovered Walter Mallott who was now apologizing and

trying to help the young man out of the pool.

Derek gave a sigh as the two men quickly ran towards him. They seemed quite

determined to do what they were hired to do. The recently assigned bodyguard of

Garrett and Taylor Law realized that this was not going to be an easy assignment at all.

The first man to approach was the bigger one of the two. His blonde hair was in a

ponytail and he wore a black T-shirt under his grey suit. The detective hoped that his

martial arts training would be enough to handle the situation as the henchman charged

at him.

Quickly, the detective sidestepped the attacker and sent a stiff ridge-hand to the throat. The attacker's feet lifted from underneath him and he landed onto the wet ground coughing.

The second attacker sent a wild punch through the air. Derek ducked and sent his fist into the guy's kidneys. Though he winced with pain, the henchman returned with a back fist catching Derek in the jaw. The detective staggered backwards from the blow alone.

"Damn!" He muttered holding his jaw. "That hurt!"

He looked up to find the man coming in for another attack. This time, he went on the offensive. He spun and sent a back kick into the man's mid-section stopping him in his tracks. He then sent a punch into the guy's jaw. The henchman fell unconscious. Derek turned as the bigger attacker stood to his feet, shaking off the effects of the clothesline.

Infuriated, he screamed as he charged. Derek hunched down and lowered his shoulder catching the stocky man. He lifted his body vaulting the man up and over. The attacker crashed into the waiter attempting to exit the pool. An eruption of water went high into air as they fell in and sprayed bystanders.

Derek comforted his jaw as he grabbed the collar of Mallott's polo shirt. "It's time to go," and he shoved the former sales manager towards the glass patio doors leading into the hotel.

The detective's pager chimed. Derek quickly withdrew it and looked at the message across the display. He concluded that he had to make one stop before securing Mallott at the beach house. He realized that he should first secure the person

he was protecting, but decided that Mallott's safety was in no more jeopardy than a nun

in a convent. In fact, he knew that where they were going all eyes would be focused on

Walter Mallott.

He returned the pager to the belt clip as Mallott looked back at the two women he

attempted to court. They smiled as he waved feverishly at them. Derek looked back to

find the henchman slowly crawling out of the pool. He sent another shove into Mallott

in hopes that he would quicken his pace.

"Don't even think about it."

Chapter Five

"I like minorities," Mallott whispered. "Really I do, but I'm a little nervous about this."

Derek smiled as the glass door of Buzz Cutts closed behind them. "Don't worry about it. You're safe here," he re-assured. "As long as you look like you want a haircut."

He could feel Mallott tensing up and it made him smile with satisfaction. He looked around the barbershop to find the entire staff of six, each wearing their neatly pressed blue smocks with the Buzz Cutts logo, occupied with customers and a waiting room of others to follow. All of them were bobbing their heads to Usher's "Yeah" which played loudly throughout the establishment. The setting reminded him of his days as a child. His father would often bring him to Buzz Cutts, the foremost authority in urban lifestyle and premiere hairstyling. The thirty minute haircut was a grooming necessity he loathed until high school.

The closest barber to him was a hefty size Hispanic by the name of Omar Gonzales. Omar was a former sheriff's deputy and went from patrolling the local prisons to enforcing the peace at the barbershop. His authority had became so popular that crime within the strip mall that housed Buzz Cutts was at an all-time low.

Next to Omar was Andre Lover, Buzz Cutt's resident comedian. During the summer he worked at Buzz Cutts, but in the fall he was a commuter student at Old Dominion University majoring in business. He was also the starting point guard for the university's basketball team. From what Derek knew of Andre, the young barber was unfortunately from the wrong side of the tracks. He lived in a seedy part of Norfolk. His father was in jail for armed robbery and his mother wandered the streets looking for her "sugar daddy". Working for Buzz Cutts reinforced his desire to be somebody and his determination to succeed.

In the middle were the two brothers, Paxton and Arturo Glidden. Together, they were the most popular and requested barbers Buzz Cutts had to offer. They were known throughout the surrounding neighborhood as "G-Love" and "G-Money", respectively.

Underneath the blue smock, "G-Money" was sharply dressed. His bald head and black leather shoes shined under the florescent ceiling lights. His silk tie was crisply tied and his gold cufflinks glistened. He looked like he would be more in his element at Wall Street rather than the urban barbershop.

His brother, "G-Love" was Buzz Cutts' Don Juan. At twenty-eight, he still retained his baby face-like traits and often used those attributes to sway the young, and sometimes older, women of the neighborhood. With so many interested and willing women, he usually carried two cell phones to handle the influx of calls. Though his counterparts ogled at the women that often accompanied "G-Love", they were glad not to be in his shoes. It would only be a matter of time, before someone's boyfriend or husband became the wiser.

Jamal Thompson was the fifth barber Derek looked at. Besides the owner, he was the oldest barber there. He was a Gulf War veteran who had retired from the Army and chose to relax. When he came into Buzz Cutts for a haircut, he and the owner spent a day just talking and Jamal soon realized that despite its surroundings, the barbershop was a peaceful environment. He asked the owner for a job and soon put his Army past behind him. The younger barbers nicknamed him "Pretty Boy" because of his caramel colored skin and well-built body, but they knew of the ugliness he ran away from and did everything they could to ensure that Buzz Cutts remained as his safe haven.

He saw the person who paged him. It was a man he considered to be his uncle. The barber was a fairly broad shouldered, dark skinned man with a snow-white goatee and a few wrinkles. The curly hair that cascaded the sides of his head matched the facial hair. Like "G-Money", his light blue barbershop uniform was pressed and his shoes were polished. His name was Clarence "Slappy" Cutter, one of the remaining founders and now sole proprietor of Buzz Cutts.

Buzz Cutts was started in 1965 by "Slappy's" uncle and father. Being a capable and eager entrepreneur, Slappy took over when he was twenty-seven. Through hard work, perseverance and a little creative advertising, he was able to generate four other Buzz Cutts satellites throughout Hampton Roads, each with a staff of six barbers, relishing in the idea of a base salary with commission, full health benefits, and "G-Money's" 401k retirement plan.

"Come on over here boy," Slappy yelled out acknowledging the detective's presence. "I have sumthin' for ya."

Derek pointed towards the soft plush chairs against the wall and motioned for Mallott to have a seat. Mallott looked around to find that he was still being watched. He decided to take a seat in the far corner against the soda machine. Derek shook his head. He knew that the neighborhood had a way of intimidating people, but it never crept into the barbershop. Slappy firmly believed that the Lord made every person equal, and that each individual had a right to share in the glory provided. Mallott was as safe as a blade of grass in a field.

The detective walked over to the gray haired barber and smiled. "You guys seem busy today?"

"Slappy" laughed as he continued grooming his patron who was reading the day's paper. The sole owner of Buzz Cutts usually sat in the back corner of the barbershop and fiddled with paperwork. For him to join his employees in the day-to-day duties of cutting hair only confirmed his earlier observation that they were extremely busy. "Summer is in full swing, not to mention it's payday. Everybody wants to look good for sumthin'."

"So, why the page?"

"I asked him to," came a voice from behind the newspaper.

It took him a moment to recognize the voice. He had not heard it for over five years. To confirm his suspicions, he grabbed the newspaper and yanked it downwards. He smiled upon recognition.

"Uncle Reggie?"

Reginald Logan looked at his best friend's son. "My goodness. You have grown up into a fine young man." He said as he cocked his head to the side.

"Don't jive like that man. You said that the last time I saw you."

Reginald gave a sharp nod. "I still mean it."

Slappy sent a flat hand against the side of Reginald's head. "Sit still Reggie, before you get a George Jefferson."

Both Derek and Reggie chuckled at Slappy's warning. "The last time we talked, you were in Philly. You were finally settling down in a two-story brick house in the suburbs."

Uncle Reggie smiled. "I did. Beautiful home, but with this new promotion from the bureau. I'm never there to enjoy it."

"So how long are you in town?" Derek asked. "Since the bureau has you bouncing from place to place."

"I should be here for a while," Reginald answered. "I'm on assignment."

"What's up?"

"Sorry, Derek, but it's classified. You know the deal. Special Agent in Charge, special information you can't share."

"Yeah, that James Bond shit," Slappy interjected. "Reggie's lips have been sealed so much, all he has is a mustache and a chin."

"Don't listen to him," Reginald stated. "Slappy's been cuttin' hair for so long, some of that hair grease has gotten into his brain."

Derek shook his head with a smile. Reginald Logan and his father grew up together in Philadelphia and served in Vietnam. Reginald was a fairly bulky individual with dark skin. His father told him that Reginald was the captain of his high school wrestling team and often worked out. His brown eyes could be cold and yet still warm the heart. He was a ladies' man and yet was able to keep his vanity at bay. His folly was the immaculate wardrobe, which represented the very image of the FBI. His newly appointed status of Special Agent in Charge was respected, as well as warranted.

After Vietnam, his father and Reginald went their separate ways. Every so often they would contact each other, but each meeting was short lived. When his mother died, Reginald did make it a point to spend as much time with his best friend and his family. It was during that time Reginald and Derek had bonded. A bond that was stronger than any friendship.

"So what are you doing tonight?" Reginald asked. "I thought maybe we could go out and do the dinner thing."

Derek looked over at Mallott who was shifting in his chair. Dinner was tempting, but he thought better of it. "Sorry, Reggie, but I have a little assignment of my own."

"The white bread?" Reginald asked.

Derek nodded. "I'm his bodyguard."

"A bodyguard? What happened to becoming a lawyer?"

Derek shook his head aware of the direction the conversation was about to take. "That's my father's dream. Not mine."

Slappy trimmed the hairline on the back of Reginald's neck. "Your father saved both of our asses from the Viet Cong. When you decided to move to Virginia, we promised him that we would keep an eye on you. He only wants the best for you. After all, he helped in creating you. You should try to respect his wishes from time to time."

"If I was to respect my father's wishes. I'd be living a lie, and my grandfather insisted that above all else, be true to yourself."

"Your grandfather was a very smart man," Reginald said. "And you're wise to follow his advice. However, I'm sure your father's intentions are valid."

"So you say, but until he tells me that himself, and convinces me otherwise, I will continue living the way I deem satisfactory to me."

"You betta check yaself." Slappy interrupted. "Your father provides the roof over your head and that hundred thousand dollar car you drive."

"I check myself every time I look in a mirror. And for your information, I pay my father rent, and I'll continue to drive the Ferrari until I can afford my own car."

Reginald reached out and grabbed Derek's hand. "Listen Derek. We don't want to argue with you. I don't approve of your father's line of work myself, but I respect him. He wants what is best for you, because he knows that is what your mother would want."

"How would my father know what my mother would want? He was always off

on a business trip for my grandfather. He doesn't know me or my sisters."

"But your sisters are making an effort to give him a chance. Why won't you?"

"As far as I'm concerned, he had his chance when my mother died," and he

closed his eyes and sighed. "I'm sorry. I shouldn't take my anger out on you."

"It's okay," Reginald replied. "Believe it or not, Slappy and I are on your side."

Derek looked at his watch. He had to get Mallott secured at the beach house.

"Listen fellas. I have to go, but call me later and I promise we'll do lunch."

"Is that cool with you Slappy?" Reginald asked.

"Joe Cool."

"Then I'll see you soon," Derek stated. "Hell. I'll even treat."

Slappy slapped Reginald's shoulder. "Hear that? The boy gets a job and now he

thinks he can buy the world."

"Hey Slappy, look at it this way. They should be supportin' us anyway," and the

two of them laughed.

Derek shook his head and began his way out of the barbershop. He could see

Mallott scrambling to his feet and racing towards the glass door. He took one final

glance at the two men who made it their business to make sure that he was provided

for. No matter what he thought, there was a reason his father chose them to be his

guardians. Their integrity and their passion for life rivaled his mother's very essence.

He missed his mother and often wondered if his father was being over-protective by

employing them, or had a foresight to know what his son really needed.

<u>**Chapter Six**</u>:

The Ferrari rolled to a standstill on the cobblestone driveway. Derek turned

off the vehicle and as he opened the door to the Italian import, he could hear the loud

music blaring throughout the beach house. He got out of the car wondering if

Courtney ignored his plea for no wild parties. Though his beach house was isolated

from his neighbors, he did not need to provide them with a reason to start complaining.

He heard the passenger side open and watched Mallott get out of the car. He

stared in awe at the beach house. He remembered that he had the same reaction when

his father first brought him here and told him that this was his new residence.

"Is this where I'm going to be staying?" Mallott asked.

"Only until the U.S. Marshal can pick you up," and Derek began to relay the

ground rules of protection. "But until they do; you are not allowed to look out of a

window, call anybody, or go outside. The only way I can guarantee your safety is for

you to follow those three simple rules. Do we have an understanding?"

Mallott pondered the thought as he closed the door to the import. He was

distracted when the front door of the beach house opened. A blonde girl wearing a red bikini and holding a squirt gun ran out laughing. Another girl with black hair and a black bikini quickly followed after her with a large rifle-like water gun.

"Ladies?" Derek said as the first girl ran past him. She turned and fired a stream of water in defense. The girl in the black two-piece swimsuit that followed after her, stopped, and fired a shot from the rifle filled with water. The water caught Derek full in the chest.

The two girls stopped, realizing what they had done. They lowered their weapons with apologetic faces. "Sorry Mr. Chase," said the girl in the black bikini.

Derek held up the tie that dripped with water. He accepted the apology with a nod and a smile. "Normally, I'd like to get wet without my clothes, but I guess I can let this one slide."

The girl in the red bikini kissed him on the cheek. "Oh thank you Mr. Chase." She smiled coyly. "That Courtney has been keeping you all to herself. It's nice to finally meet you. My name is Alexis," and she pointed to the woman in the black bikini. "That's Indigo, we call her Indy."

"Nice to meet you both." Derek said. Including Courtney, there were seven models staying at the beach house, and though he didn't know them by face, he knew their names. Because he just stumbled upon Alexis and Indigo, he knew Valerie, Tasha, Brooke, and Mei Ling were the only ones left to meet.

"Why don't you meet us at the Jacuzzi tonight," Indy began. "A bunch of us are going to be there just hangin' out."

"Not to mention," Alexis interjected. "You'll get a chance to meet the rest of the models of Glamour Girls Incorporated."

"I'll make sure I'm not wearing clothes this time."

"Good," Indy replied and then she gave a seductive smile Derek often saw on the front cover of magazines. "Cuz', we won't be."

Derek thought back to when he had seen a smile like that earlier today. It was when he saw Courtney during her photo shoot on his deck. He concluded that each of the seven Glamour Girl models were groomed to master that same seductive smile. Because he knew Courtney so well, he had learned one thing about that devilish smile; it meant trouble was not far behind.

"See ya tonight, Mr. Chase." Alexis said.

It did not take long for Derek to make a decision as he contemplated the consequences of fulfilling a lifelong fantasy. The girls went around the side of the house and ran down the sandy trail that led towards the beach as Mallott stared in awe.

"If they're staying here," Mallott began. Derek looked over and could see the drool beginning to form. "I'll follow any rule you have."

Derek raised an eyebrow. "Yeah, I bet."

It took an hour before Derek found Courtney to find out what was going on. Courtney relayed that she and Ms. Lockehart had been scouring the town setting up photo shoots at different locations. Courtney also informed Derek that the girls had been working hard for a month straight and probably needed a much deserved break.

Hence, the water gun fight through the house. Derek accepted Courtney's rationalization, as well as her vow, that the girls would be more courteous in the future.

He was now in the loft of his beach house where his computer was. He was signing on to the Internet to see if he had gotten any messages from any of his friends from around the globe. For the most part, it was for recreational purposes, but from time to time, he used the Internet to gather useful information.

While he listened to the modem dial out, he looked over on the side of the desk. Sitting in between the computer and a picture of him and his three sisters, was a leather scrapbook bound by a faded white ribbon. He reached for a leather scrapbook and undid the ribbon. He opened it and the past came alive.

"You can't have it!"

"Give it back to me! It's my teddy bear!"

"I want it."

"Now, now children," she said. "What's all the yelling about?"

"Derek won't give me Mr. Sniffles!"

He looked at her as she knelt down between her two children. Her long black hair shined and her light complexion accented her angelic face. Her smile was comforting and her voice was soft and loving. "Derek, why won't you give Allyson Mr. Sniffles?"

"Allyson always gets everything! I never get anything!"

"Ah," his mother responded. "That's not true. Your father and I give you anything you ask for."

"I asked for a teddy bear. How come I didn't get a teddy bear and she did?"

She rubbed her child's back affectionately. "Well, Mr. Sniffles protects Allyson from all those monsters under her bed. Mr. Sniffles is brave and strong like you. Your father and I thought that because you are a brave, strong boy you did not need a teddy bear. Now, if you want we can go to the store tomorrow and get you your very own teddy bear, and you can play with him all day if you like. But, before we do, you have to let me know if there are monsters under your bed. Are there monsters under your bed?"

He shook his head.

"Do you really think that a big, strong, brave boy like yourself needs a teddy bear to protect him?"

He shook his head again.

She smiled and hugged him. "I didn't think so either. Tell you what, why don't you give Allyson Mr. Sniffles and you two can come downstairs and help me bake some cookies. Would you like that?"

They both nodded and Derek handed the brown bear to his sister.

"What do you say?" his mother asked.

"I'm sorry."

She kissed him on the cheek. "That's my brave son. C'mon lets go make some cookies."

He turned the page and read the newspaper clippings he had read so many times before. Each sentence made the lump in his throat that much harder to swallow.

The wooden plane zig-zagged and swerved through the air as the front door rang. He landed the wooden flyer on the floor beside his other toys as the maid answered the door. He looked up and saw Uncle Slappy.

"Uncle Slappy!" he yelled and he left the plane running for the front door.

"Hey there!" Slappy said smiling. He knelt down and lifted the boy in the air and into his arms. "How's my favorite nephew doing?"

"Fine."

"Are you still practicing your karate?"

He nodded. "Yes sir! I'm on basic form four now."

"Good," Slappy responded. "Keep it up. One day you can participate in the tournaments."

"Not if I can help it," came a voice. "Even if I have to fight Roo himself." He looked behind him and saw his father coming out of the study. He was smoking his pipe. Compared to Slappy, his father was a much bigger man whose very essence commanded respect. "How are you doing Slappy? Are you and Reggie enjoying your vacation at my expense?"

"I wish it were under better circumstances," Slappy responded. His tone was more serious than earlier. He lowered Derek to the ground and smacked his rear. "Derek, why don't you go into the kitchen and let me have a few moments alone with your father."

"Yes sir," and with that Derek scurried away into the kitchen. He quickly stopped and peered around the corner.

"What's going on Slappy?"

Slappy took in a deep breath and lowered his head. "Tom, we heard some talk in the town about Kara. I'm afraid there's been an accident."

His father's knees almost gave way as he stumbled towards the door frame. He clutched his heart. "Oh my God."

"Her car went over a cliff, the local police are still going through the wreckage. They need you to identify the body."

"Where's Reggie?"

"He's there now, making sure the locals are not botching things up. They think it may be retaliation to her father's decision to put you in charge of the company."

"What about the baby?"

Slappy shook his head.

Derek stood out from the door frame and cocked his head to the side. It looked like his father was crying. He had never seen his father cry. "Daddy?" He asked. "Why are you crying?"

His father turned to find his son in the door frame. He took in a deep breath and went over to his son and knelt down. "Your father is very sad."

"Is it because of mommy?"

His father nodded. "Mommy is taking a little trip right now."

"Is she coming back?"

His father shook his head. He could sense the pain his father was going through and it scared him. "Not now, but one day, we'll see her again. I promise."

"Tom," Slappy started. "We gotta go."

His father looked over at Slappy with a solemn face. He took in a deep breath and swallowed as he looked back at his son. He hugged his little boy as tears rolled down his eyes. "I need you to be strong for your sisters. It's up to you and me from now on. Do you understand me?"

Derek nodded.

His father forced a smile. "Good boy, now go play and I'll be home soon."

"Yes sir."

He wiped a tear from his eye as he heard the computer welcome him to the Internet. From what he could remember, his mother's death was still a mystery to him. Somehow she lost control of her car and went over a cliff. San Pulerio Police ruled that the accident was due to poor weather conditions. Though it rained that night, it was hard for him to believe, because his mother's wreckage was found during the day; and he remembered the day as being warm and clear.

He believed that somehow, someone convinced the police not to pursue the issue any further than they did. Through some investigation of his own, he discovered that the police report was incomplete, there was no mention of a second set of tire tracks and the broken glass, possibly from a taillight a few hundred yards away from where his mother's car went off the cliff. There were rumors that the local elders were upset with his grandfather, Enrique Denteveron, and took revenge by killing the one thing he cherished more than anything else, his daughter. Of course, the opportunity for Derek to get more information about his mother's accident had presented itself once before, but his own convictions, as well as his stubborn pride, got in the way.

His ears caught the sound of a weapon being cocked behind his back. Before he could react, he was frozen by the familiar voice that began to bellow throughout the parking garage. "You always had a flare for the dramatic, eh Rookie? Drop the gun and kick it away."

Derek uncocked the weapon and slowly lowered the gun to the ground. He raised his hands as he resumed his full height and gently kicked the gun across the parking lot a few feet away from him.

"Mr. Chase," Janocky interrupted. "I believe you already know my Chief Security Advisor and personal bodyguard, Nick Letourneau."

"I should've known that it would've only been a matter of time before I ran into you again."

Nick Letourneau stepped in front of Derek and smiled. His face was haggard and his hair was mostly gray, almost white in some spots. He seemed hardened from his term in prison. Derek mocked the ex-cop's smile. "I'm getting the sense that you're not happy to see me." Letourneau said as he began frisking the detective.

"I'm not," the detective replied. "Early parole?"

Letourneau chuckled as he withdrew the pistol from the small of Derek's back. "You can say that," he said as he tossed the weapon. "Janocky heard about my situation and sent his lawyers to do some plea bargaining on my behalf."

"Another fine example of how our justice system works."

"Listen Rookie," Letourneau began. "The system fucked us both. Let's work together; we can change this city. Make the system work for us for a change."

It was Derek's turn to chuckle. "I think, I'm gonna pass on this one. Maybe some other time."

Letourneau smiled and shook his head. "You always thought you were a righteous cop. Look where it got you? I'm offering the chance to take back what's yours."

"I won't lose my soul for it."

"Think about it Mr. Chase," Janocky interjected. "With a man of your background and connections, this could be the opportunity of a lifetime."

"I'm afraid you don't know me all that well."

"On the contrary. I know more about you than you realize. You see I conducted a little investigation on my own. I know your father, Thomas Washington is the son-in-law to Enrique Denteveron. When your grandfather passed, your father inherited seventy-eight percent of the business and some of the people in your grandfather's organization were not too pleased with that decision. So, when your father decided to move the company headquarters from Columbia to the United States, it was more for personal reasons than for business politics. Join us Mr. Chase, and together we can assure the security of your grandfather's corporation and his name. We might even be able to find out who murdered your mother."

"You think by bringing my family into this will change my mind?" Derek laughed. "My father has done well thus far without you or me. And as for my

mother's killer, I'm quite capable of determining that on my own. So once again, the answer is no."

Letourneau and Janocky looked at the detective realizing that the look in his eyes was not to be swayed. Letourneau gave a humpf. "You're a stubborn bastard." He uncocked his weapon and secured it in the shoulder holster within the confines of his suit jacket. "Okay Rookie, go it alone. But I'm warning you, stay away from Janocky."

"And if I don't?"

Letourneau remained quiet and just smiled.

While investigating the murder of Sydney's sister, Tessa, he stumbled across a case file involving Thomas Janocky III and his company Griffin Securities. Believing her death to be a result of her investigation, he pursued the lead to be caught up in an intricate web of police corruption and corporate espionage. It became more complicated when Derek's mentor, Sgt. Nick Letourneau, became Janocky's personal bodyguard. To make matters worse, Letourneau was determined to exact revenge for Derek testifying against him in a case which Letourneau had murdered an unarmed Internal Affairs officer.

He took in a deep breath as he shuffled the past to the dark corners of his memory. Thomas Janocky III had been arrested and was in jail for conspiracy to commit murder and corporate espionage. In the process of defending himself during a home invasion, Derek killed Nick Letourneau, thus ending his self-persecution.

The computer chimed alerting him that there was electronic mail waiting. He would have to think about his personal inquiry into his mother's death some other time. Derek's fingers danced along the computer keyboard as he typed in commands. The computer screen then flickered to a screen of a mailbox and dark blue lettering that said: MAILBAG. A cartoon postman then walked onto the screen and put an envelope in the mailbox. The cartoon image then waved at Derek and walked off. Underneath the marquee MAILBAG, was the word NEWMAIL flashing in red letters.

Derek's hand went from the keyboard to the mouse. He guided the arrow on the computer to the flashing word. He then clicked the button on the mouse twice and the screen flickered to a picture of an envelope. Printed on the envelope was a list of people who had sent him electronic mail. He scanned the list of four people trying to determine which was the most important. He decided to pull up the E-mail from his sister Victoria in Canada,

Out of four children, Victoria was the oldest followed by his sister Allyson and then himself. The youngest, was his sister Crystal, who was continuing her education at Ithaca College in New York. She was majoring in Business with a Minor in Law. She followed her father's example in hopes of one day running the family business.

Allyson was the quiet one of the family. She was an elementary school teacher with a firm belief that if she could change the lives of children while they were still young, she would have a foundation to build a better society. Derek often teased his sister, calling her Don Quixote dreaming the impossible dream. However, she was just a stubborn as he was, so Derek knew that in the battle of changing society for the better, Allyson was the best candidate to put up a good fight.

Victoria, or Tory as she was known, was working as a research consultant for one of their father's companies in Canada. She happily accepted her father's attempts of spoiling her. However, she retained her "work hard" attitude, which helped her to obtain a Magna Cum Laude status when she graduated from UCLA. Because she was in Canada, she kept in touch with Derek and the rest the family through electronic mail, and despite their opposing viewpoints in regards to their father, Victoria understood, loved and supported her brother.

Derek frowned. Victoria's e-mail was alerting him that she was currently in Connecticut visiting Allyson and Crystal, however she and his father would be in Virginia Beach in October. It was June now, giving Derek five months to concoct a schedule that would keep him and his father apart as much as possible.

The second e-mail was from a pen pal in Utah relaying a hello and the third was from a person he met a week ago in "The Forum", an area on the Internet where people from all over the country could write to each other live. Sometimes, it got confusing watching sentences that did not make any sense, but it was fun nonetheless. Her screen name was Deelicious, and from the conversation they had that night, she was trying to get him to visit her in Maryland to prove her screen name true. The e-mail in front of him was more or less the same plea for a chance encounter.

Maybe some other time. Derek thought to himself.

Derek took in a deep breath and ignored the other electronic messages. He would

get to them later. He closed his mailbox. He sat back in his chair as the star field

simulation screen saver appeared. He closed his eyes feeling the urge to take a nap.

His interaction with Glamour Girls Incorporated and Walter Mallott left him

exhausted. He smiled at the thought that Walter was safely tucked away in a locked

room with cable television. He complained to Derek for not being in the Jacuzzi with

the models of Glamour Girls Incorporated. Despite the complaints, Derek was

satisfied that it was the right decision.

He heard a door opening behind him, snatching him from the brink of

unconsciousness. He turned to find Courtney standing in the doorway.

"Whatcha doin'?" Courtney asked stepping into the den. The dim light revealed

that she was wearing a red robe with her blonde hair up in a ponytail. Derek observed

that despite her taxing day, she looked relaxed.

"Just checking my email."

Courtney stepped up between Derek and the computer. "Well, if you can pull

yourself away from surfing the net, the others are waiting in the Jacuzzi."

"Oh really?" Derek replied and then he thought of what Indy said earlier when

they were in the driveway. "Are they wearing bathing suits or are they just buffing it?"

Courtney smiled and she sat down straddling his legs. The robe loosely flopped

over his knees. "They're wearing the same thing that I'm wearing under this robe."

"And what would that be?" Derek asked reaching for the drawstring of the robe.

Courtney quickly slapped his hand with a smile and stood up. "There's only one way you're gonna find out," and she went for the door.

Derek spun the chair leaping at her. In one step, he was upon her. He encircled his arm around her and lifted her off the ground. "Oh no you don't," he said.

Courtney giggled as he spun her around. He then sat her down in a large soft cushioned chair and hovered over her. "You think you're so tough, don'tcha?" she said.

Derek raised an eyebrow. "Yeah, I do."

"Well, I'm tougher than you are." She challenged.

"I don't think so."

"How do you figure?"

Derek looked deep into Courtney's eyes. "You wanna kiss me, don'tcha?"

"No I don't," she giggled. "What made you think that?"

Derek leaned closer. Maybe Dr. Gellar was right. Maybe he should let love run its course. He could smell the faint perfume radiating from her body. The sweet scent invigorated his lungs. He fought the urge to yell out his true feelings, afraid fate would step in and provide another reason to remain isolated. "Your eyes say different." he said smoothly as the back of his hand went up and caressed the side of her face. "They say, 'I can't help but be in love with this man.' They say, 'I want to steal a kiss from his lips.'"

"Then what do you suggest I do, if my eyes are saying all this?"

"Give in."

Courtney looked at him as he came closer. He could see that she was calculating the situation in her mind. He wondered if she could deny the feelings that she had buried deep inside her? Could she give in? What would happen if she did? It felt so wrong, and yet so right. Their friendship would change and the change would either bring them closer, or tear them apart. Could he risk all they had built together as friends? Their lips merged.

After a moment she broke away with a half-hearted smile. "Derek, I can't. Not now," and with that she sat up.

He backed off, but took a more verbal approach.

"What happened between us?" he asked.

"I don't know what you mean."

"Well, after you came back from California, it was different. You were distant. And when we talked," and he gave a sigh. "I don't know. I can't put it in words, it's like you shut me out. Before you left, you and I were very close. We made promises to each other, we were going to be together. You said it was our dream."

"Well," she began. She stood up from the chair. Her tone was slightly defensive. "I realized that sometimes dreams don't come true."

"What are you trying to say?"

"It's better that I don't discuss it with you now."

"Then when?" His tone was now getting defensive. The passion he felt was fostering his curiosity. "Next time you're in town? Next month? Next year? Tell me Courtney, what's up?"

She looked at him. He could see tears welling up in her eyes. "Have you ever

thought that maybe I just don't love you anymore?"

He was silent. She looked at him. There was regret in her face. Saddened, she

closed her eyes and fell into the soft cushion of the chair. His heart thumped hard

against his chest. Though part of him was relieved that he would spare her from the

fate of those he had loved previously, he still had not expected that response and the

angered tone that accompanied it.

"I'm sorry," she said. "I didn't mean to-

"It's okay," he interrupted. The lump in his throat made it hard for him to talk.

"One of us had to wake up sometime," and he walked out of the den.

<u>**Chapter Seven**</u>:

The beach house was dark as Derek sat in the kitchen. He had changed into a denim shirt and a pair of jeans. He sat at the island nursing a bottle of beer. Though he was comfortable in his choice of attire, his earlier conversation with Courtney disturbed him. He believed that there was something more than what she was letting on. They had formed a bond in high and it survived his father's globe trekking and his enrollment into Ithaca. He took in deep breath thinking back to the time before she left to become a model and his wariness of seeing her dreams and ambitions of becoming a model fall to the wayside. He thought about the one carat diamond ring buried underneath the stairs leading to the beach sand and wrestled with the notion of burying his feelings for Courtney alongside it.

The kitchen light came on startling him. He looked over to find a dark haired woman standing by the refrigerator wearing nothing more than a purple teddy. He could not help but see through the material.

"Indy," Derek began trying to keep his voice to a whisper. "It's late. What are you doing up?".

"I couldn't sleep," she replied moving closer. As she walked behind him, she slid her hand down his back. "And I saw you walk into the kitchen, so I thought I would see what you were up to."

Derek looked at her; half curious as to what her true intentions were, the other half wondering whether or not to believe it. "Just gathering my thoughts before I go to bed."

Indy looked at the bottle of beer he was nursing. "Courtney?"

He took a swig of beer.

She shook her head. "Sometimes, Courtney doesn't really know what's best for her."

He scratched at the goatee. His curiosity got the better of him. "And what would that be?"

"A big, strong, handsome, caring man," she answered. Her hands were slithering around his body exploring his figure. Her perfume was intoxicating as the beer he held in his hand. He could feel the warmth of her breath on the back of his neck. "Someone like yourself."

"How would you know?"

She giggled. "Girl talk," she answered and she leaned closer to his ear. He turned slightly to see that her tanned breasts were exposed for him to see. "After all, Courtney and I share the same taste. If you know what I mean."

"Is that so?"

Her tongue lightly caressed the side of his cheek. "Ever since we got here, she has not been able to stop talking about you. I want to know if all she says is true."

He took a sip from the bottle and looked at her dead in the eye. "Take her word for it."

She sent a seductive smile. His challenge would not go undaunted. "Oh, Mr. Chase, I've always been a person who likes to find out things on their own. That is if you think you can handle what I have to offer."

"And what would that be?"

"A night in which Courtney Lathaye is nothing more than a memory."

Despite his conscience, he contemplated the consequences. Her body was well built and proportioned in all the right places. She truly deserved the term model. He sensed that her spirit was wild and uncontrollable. That stirred a desire burrowed deep inside his psyche. However, he decided that a one night stand would do more harm than good. "I'm sorry," he answered and he took another swig of his beer. "I think I'll pass this time."

Indy smiled as she invaded his personal space. Her perfume was sweet and her breath was warm. The hairs on the back of his neck stood upright when her breast rubbed up against his chest. She was slowly taking in his scent like a wounded dog. He stiffened as she softly kissed him on the lips.

She stepped back and smiled. "Too bad."

She pulled the strap to her teddy. The middle came apart and the ends briefly fell to the sides of her breasts before continuing straight down to the floor. He took in a deep breath, and an eye-full, as she stood there naked. Her sun bronzed body looked creamy, as if she had been made with milk and honey. Her long black hair gently brushed against her back like a cape. Her breasts were round and her nipples were firm and taut. They would reach out to him slightly as she breathed. He assumed they were real. If it had been plastic surgery, he couldn't tell the difference. He scanned the ripples of her abdomen that had been through intense conditioning to find a small diamond cleverly tucked away in her navel. Below that, was a neatly trimmed runway of dark peach fuzz that undoubtedly would be the key to opening Pandora's Box. Her legs were shapely and smooth and he could sense their yearning for the chance to run free. Everything about her was flawless and she was flaunting it.

She continued to taunt him. "I was hoping that I could talk you into a massage under the moonlight. " and with that, she slowly backed her way into the foyer.

"The answer is still no."

"I'll be on the beach if your change your mind."

He watched her as she walked into the large foyer. She winked in hopes that he would take pursuit. He took another swig, finishing off the beer, and stood from the island in the kitchen. She turned towards the front door in anticipation that he would follow her to the beach underneath the Virginia Beach moonlight. Her excitement suddenly changed to fear. She froze as she quickly focused on a dark figure at the front door. It loomed only a few feet away, and she gasped realizing that a pistol in the figure's hand was aimed at her.

"Say goodnight Indigo."

A soft pop echoed throughout the foyer. Derek looked on from the island as he saw Indy's head jerk backwards. Her arms and legs went limp. He reached the edge of the foyer as Indy's body slowly turned sideways. He could see the passion for life leaving Indy's eyes as she fell to the floor.

"Indy!" He yelled running into the foyer.

Derek turned and was startled to see a dark clad figure standing in the foyer. He then noticed that the assailant had a pistol with a silencer aimed at him. He could see the dark figure squeezing the trigger. His teeth clenched as he closed his eyes in anticipation of the silent pop. Instead, he heard a loud click. He opened his eyes to find the dark figure struggling with the pistol. The gun had jammed.

The clip fell onto the floor as the dark figure cocked the hammer back releasing the jammed bullet. The mystery guest quickly began loading another cartridge of bullets into the pistol as a light came on.

"Hey, what's going on?" Mallott screamed out. He was standing in the doorway to his room wearing a pink bathrobe. There were soft mumbles of protest from the sleeping beauties arranged on the carpet. They were pulling the covers of their sleeping bags over their eyes. "People are trying to sleep!"

"Everybody stay down!" Derek ordered running across the foyer into the living room. The assailant took aim at Mallott and fired as Derek dove across the beige sectional sofa tackling his pink robed guest. The bullet shattered one of the twin designer lamps that sat on each side of the curved sofa. The models of Glamour Girls Incorporated began screaming upon the realization of what was taking place.

Exposed, the dark figure fired as it retreated outside. Bullets ricocheted harmlessly against the wall. Once the firing ceased, Derek stood up from the protection of the sofa and followed after the figure. He ran through the living room and into the foyer as the group of girls began weeping at the sight of their fallen friend and co-worker.

He stepped out of the house and did a quick scan of the area. He saw nothing. He cautiously walked onto the cobblestone driveway scanning the area straining his ears to listen, but he could only hear the crashing of the ocean against the sand. The dark figure had become a part of the night scenery. He stepped in the middle of the driveway and slowly surveyed his surroundings. The only thing he could see was the Ferrari and a variety of vegetation his father insisted would beautify the landscape of the beach house. It served as the perfect shroud for Indy's murderer to escape.

He heard an engine revving to life at the end of the driveway towards the street. He ran towards the sound as he heard tires clawing for traction. He ran out on the street and was quickly blinded by bright lights. He shielded his eyes from the light as a car quickly thundered towards him. Out of survival instincts alone, and with no time to dive out of the way, he jumped upwards, crashing onto the hood of the car. The impact caused him to bounce against the windshield and he could feel it crack against his body. He rolled off the side of the fleeing vehicle and landed hard onto the pavement. He laid there motionless listening to the car engine fade off into the night. He fought the black shroud beginning to overtake him as he faintly heard Courtney's yell of anguish. He fought to get up, but the darkness prevailed. The chances of catching

Indy's killer had faded away with his consciousness.

**He closed his eyes from the hospital's bright light, which was adding fuel to

the headache he retained from his one-on-one face off with some car

manufacturer's idea of the perfect automobile.** He felt like an extra in the Stephen

King novel "Christine". He rubbed the back of his neck hoping that the pain would go

away.

"You should be dead, you know."

He looked up towards the voice to find a friend from the Virginia Beach Police

Department. He had been a cop once, and that had led him down a path of unforgiving

persecution for doing the job he swore to uphold. Despite his past and current

relationship with the department, Elizabeth Marie Companstella remained true to him.

He acknowledged her presence with a nod and braced himself for the lecture she had

prepared.

"I don't want to hear it."

"Hear what?" She asked.

He could hear the sarcasm as he looked at her. He cocked his head to the side.

Normally, she would be making her father and her older brothers proud by wearing her

uniform, otherwise she would be in a pair of jeans and a somewhat loose fitting tank

top. Instead, this half Hispanic, half African-American woman, who had taken on the role normally reserved for the men in her family, was wearing a tight blue mini skirt and a pink halter top. Her black fish-net stockings were only complimented by the pink high heeled pumps. He was used to the natural beauty of her face with her rounded cheeks and slightly flattened nose, but tonight it seemed perverted with the painted on make-up. It was overkill. Her normally curly hair had been straightened and bundled tightly into a pony-tail. The only thing he did recognize was the badge dangling between her breasts.

"Hear whatever motherly advice you're about to tell me."

"You of all people should know I would never consider myself as your mother."

He gave a sheepish grin. "I didn't realize Halloween was going to be early this year." He said taking in her appearance again. "I would have brought some candy."

She smirked at him and responded. "Smart ass. Vice needed some help tonight, so I volunteered. I heard what happened over the radio and came over to check on you."

"Oh." He started. The headache had lessened to a mild thumping against his forehead. He smiled flirtatiously. "Well, maybe later on, when you're not on duty, you could come over and-

"Have you love me and leave me like you did last time? Or have you re-thought your decision to keep me at bay, even though everyone you say you care about is dead?"

He swallowed hard remembering the forbidden relationship they shared.

"Sometimes, you need to have the desire to want to do something." she advised. Her voice then softened. "You'd be surprised at what you can do when you want something bad enough."

He looked up at her as she stood behind him. He wiped the corners of his mouth with his napkin and stood up from the table. He took a step into her personal space and took her hand. Her skin was soft and her perfume was sweet and invigorating.

"You know Elizabeth," he began. "That almost sounded like a subtle hint."

"Elizabeth?" she asked. "No witty nicknames Mr. Chase?"

"Not tonight."

She smiled. "Well, you're the detective. All the evidence is there in front of you. All you have to do is look for the obvious."

They leaned closer towards each other and their lips merged. They hungrily kissed each other as her arms separated from his hands. They slowly traced the curvatures of his back as she embraced him. His hands worked their way from her shoulders to her buttocks as he pressed up against her firm body. His hands then followed her spine upwards to her neck. He cradled the back of her head letting her long black hair run through his fingers. She could feel his body responding to hers. Their lips parted and they looked at each other.

"This could get complicated," she warned.

"Well, Ms. Companstella." He smiled. "You're the police officer, handle the situation."

She looked into his eyes and threw caution to the wind. Her lips joined with his determined to fulfill a fantasy long awaited.

She slept peacefully snuggling up against his warm chest. *He held her firmly as he re-played the night's happenings. They made love twice that night, the second time more intoxicating and relentless than the first. Derek committed every detail of Elizabeth's body and how she moved to memory.*

He thought of her words and her kisses, remembering that it had been a long time since somebody made him feel like a special part of their life. He took in a deep breath as his hand caressed her shoulder. Her skin was so soft that it almost felt like silk. He realized that she was softer than her appearance led on as he lightly kissed her on the forehead.

"Elizabeth, I think-

"I know Derek," she interrupted. Her voice was still weak. "You don't have to explain. I know."

"E. It's not that I don't want to."

She pretended to smile. "But you won't. It's how you survive."

He kissed her on the forehead. "I will always be there when you need me."

.He took in a deep breath still recoiling from her last statement. "That hurt."

"Well, you deserve it." She retorted as she walked up. She kissed him passionately on the lips. Satisfied, she slowly broke away from him resuming her professional demeanor.

"What was that for?" He asked. He was confused.

"I needed to get that out of my system." She answered. He could see a tear forming as she continued. "I can still care about you if I'm going to be your friend. I just can't love you."

"E," he began. "I'm sorry."

She wiped a tear from her eye as the door to the room opened. He immediately recognized the brown hair with the blonde streaks flowing loosely across the doctor's shoulders. She had changed from the short sleeve blue hospital shirt she wore during brunch to a green one. It was wrinkled with a few dots of dried blood that survived the hot water wash of the hospital's laundry room. He watched how her smooth cheek bones hugged the curves of her face as she smiled. Her eyes searched his for an explanation.

"Good evening Mr. Chase."

"Good evening Dr. Gellar."

E took a step backwards into a corner as Dr. Gellar looked at her clipboard. "It says you were hit by a car?"

"Yes, I was."

She scribbled a message on her clipboard before flipping a page over. "Your x-rays came back okay. Nothing broken, but you will be sore for a week or two.

Though, I say this for my health, get plenty of rest; and may I suggest a change of profession?"

"Noted. May I go now?"

"Yes," she answered handing him the clipboard. "Just sign these documents and you'll be on your way."

He wanted to say something witty to Dr. Gellar, but resisted the temptation for E's sake. He signed the clipboard and handed it back to her.

"Thanks Doc."

"No problem," she said taking the clipboard back. She reviewed the document and smiled. "But I'm sure I'll be seeing you soon enough, and probably not at brunch."

He smirked reflecting on his previous engagements with Dr. Gellar as she walked out of the room. Their few meetings were at best mild adversarial outlets of flirtation, innocent with the potential to become something much more risqué. He looked over at E who stood in the corner looking on. He could see worry in her hazel eyes. He wanted to console her and apologize for overstepping the boundaries of friendship, but it would only cause both of them more pain. He reserved the right to talk about it at another time and place when their lives would be less complicated. Instead, he chose another conversation. "Did they find out anything at the house?"

E shook her head. Her professionalism was quickly covering up her emotions. "Are you sure you turned on that hi-tech alarm system your father installed?"

"Ever since my house was broken into, I've had it on religiously. It has a timer that's set to arm at ten o'clock each night and it's on a separate generator in case there is a blackout."

"Well, I talked to one of the uniforms and he said that according to forensics, someone bypassed the alarm system."

"The only way they could do that was to know the code, but that's impossible. Only my father and I know the code."

E shrugged. "I'm only the messenger. Detectives are still looking over the house."

The door to the examination room opened with a loud boom. To his dismay, Lieutenant Terry Austin stepped in. Derek gave a moan and Austin's blue eyes glared at the detective. He rubbed the stubble around his jaw contemplating what he would say to the detective.

"Something told me it would be you." Austin began with a huff. He was a man of medium-build in his mid-forties. He was balding and the gray beard added to the look of fatigue. His face was chiseled like that of a gargoyle protecting a castle, but despite his hardened looks, he was respected by his peers and the officers in his command. He wore a sports jacket over a sweater and a pair of jeans rather than his normal S&K Men's Warehouse suit. He growled as he started his interrogation. "Would you mind telling me why there's a woman on the floor in your house with her tits hangin' all out and a bullet hole in her head?"

"I don't know," answered the detective. "But I don't think she was the target."

"What do you mean?" Austin asked.

"I'm currently protecting a federal witness until the U.S. Marshals can take him into custody."

"You're shitting me," Austin began. Derek and E both could sense the lecture that was about to follow. "You're keeping a federal witness at your house? That is the most asinine thing I ever heard of."

He interjected before the Lieutenant could continue. "Look Austin. I have a dead woman in my house, I've been ran over by a car, and I have a splitting headache. Can you please get off my back?"

"Chase. I'm not playing. You're endangering a federal witness. If something happens to him, the feds are gonna be all over your ass."

"Mallott was perfectly safe." He replied hopping off of the hospital bed and standing to his feet. His legs felt stiff.

"Yeah," Austin taunted. "A regular Fort Knox. Too bad you failed to protect that model." He then gave a low growl. "Let me make this very clear," he began. "This is now a homicide, a police matter. We will handle this. If you want to be helpful I suggest you stay out of our way."

"There's a chalk outline of a naked woman in my foyer! You stay out of my way!" His attention then diverted towards E as he immediately thought about Garrett and Taylor's star witness. In all the commotion, he had been distracted. "Where's Mallott?"

"He's in the waiting room with a uniform." E answered. "He told me that you were his bodyguard. I didn't think you would mind if I brought him along."

The stiffness in his legs lessened as blood began circulating. He walked up to E and kissed her on the cheek as Austin raised an eyebrow. "Thanks E. I owe you one."

"Yeah, I know." She interjected. She reached into her jean pocket and dangled the keys to the Ferrari in front of him. "I also took the liberty of driving your car over. Thought you might be needing it."

He took the keys from her and kissed her again on the cheek.

"What would I ever do without you?" he asked as he started for the door.

"That remains to be seen." She answered.

It took Austin a minute before he could ignore the relationship between Derek and E. He quickly yelled at the detective who was opening the heavy wooden door of the hospital room. "Chase! Let the police handle this one!"

He sighed loudly, aware that his vocal directive was in vain. Derek was already out the door.

Chapter <u>Eight</u>:

The Ferrari eased into the long driveway of Virginia Wesleyan College. With

the trees outlining the road, the setting resembled the path taken by an unsuspecting

traveler in a black and white horror movie. He looked over at Mallott. His arms were

folded across the pink robe and he was talking to himself. From what Derek could

make it out, it sounded more like complaints. Mallott would have to adjust to his new

scenery until the detective could make heads or tails of what happened at the beach

house. His home was compromised and Mallott's security had to be insured.

He dimmed the lights as he coasted towards the security gate. He hoped his

friend Donnatello was working. He and Donnatello Smith were sparring partners when

he was enrolled in Master Roo's Tang Soo Do class. Master Qui Roo was a Japanese-

Korean American well versed in five styles of martial arts. He had served with Derek's

father during Vietnam and during the war they became close friends. After the war,

Master Roo often visited his father in South America, bringing with him three boxes

from the United States and a briefcase of paperwork. With each visit, he passed down

his heritage and his martial arts to Derek and his siblings. When Derek's father briefly

moved the family to Virginia Beach, Master Roo quickly enrolled the children into his martial arts class and devoted his livelihood to his four young successors. His instruction was often interrupted by his father's constant travels. However, by the time Derek's father had most of the family business transitioned to their headquarters in Connecticut, Derek and his sister Crystal were in high school and both third degree black belts. They had surpassed Victoria and Allyson, who had decided that their social lives were too important to continue with Master Roo's grandiose plans of finding an heir for his knowledge and skills.

Just before earning his third degree black belt, Derek met Donnatello. Donnatello was a transfer student from California and a second degree black belt in Jujitsu. There was a power struggle right from the beginning and with their unbridled aggressiveness towards one another, Master Roo decided it was best to pair the two. Quite often they would leave class licking their wounds. It took a while, but their aggressiveness and strengths were channeled. It was not long before they became two of the top twenty martial artists in the state tournaments. The only person that surpassed them, was Derek's younger sister, Crystal. She was quick in learning how to channel her energy, something that took Derek and Donnatello months to learn after inflicting pain on one another.

"Where are we going?" Mallott asked. "What is this place?"

Derek noticed the familiar 1985 Mustang GT sitting beside the security check-in booth. He was in luck. Donnatello was working. "This is going to be your new home until I say otherwise."

"What?" Mallott asked. "You can't do this."

"Watch me," Derek said as he downshifted and applied the brakes. "And the same rules apply here as they did at the beach house," he then looked at Mallott remembering back to when he stepped out of his room. "Speaking of which, how did you get out of your room tonight?" he asked puzzled. "Didn't I lock you in?"

Mallott's eyes searched the scenery looking for an answer. He could not think of one. His voice quivered as the truth came out. "I picked the lock?"

"You picked the lock?"

"Well, what do you expect?" Mallott defended. "I was an accountant for a hardware store! The mechanics teach you things from time to time!"

The detective sighed silently to himself. "This is your first and last warning," and he stared at Mallott. Mallott could see the fire in his eyes. "If you ever pull another stunt like that again, I'll turn you over to Tony Cooke myself. Do you understand?"

Mallott slowly nodded.

Derek slowed the car to a halt and rolled down the window. He chuckled. "Besides, I don't think you'll be going anywhere if all you have is a pink robe."

"Hey," Mallott protested. "That's crazy!"

He ignored his comment as the security guard lowered his head into the window of the Ferrari. Derek was glad to see his friend again. However, with the recognition of the driver, Donnatello started shaking his head. His dark skinned face was a suitable contrast to the white, short sleeve uniform of campus security.

"I'm sorry," Donnatello began. His white teeth smiled at the detective mischievously. "But visiting hours were over three hours ago."

"C'mon Donnie," Derek pleaded. "I need a favor."

"When don't you need a favor?"

"That's just wrong," Derek defended. "Why you gonna treat a brotha like that?"

"Please," Donnatello began. "Who do I look like? TC from *Magnum P.I.*? I've done more favors for you than I can count on both hands."

"This'll be the last one."

"I've heard that before."

The detective almost chuckled. Donnatello was right, he had heard that one before. He looked at the security guard to find him wrestling with his conscience. After this, he would take Donnatello out for a nice night on the town with the models of Glamour Girls Incorporated. He smiled at the thought of Donnatello drooling over his half-dressed house guests.

"Look Donnie. I just need to put this guy somewhere for a couple of days. You won't even know he's here."

Donnatello looked past Derek's shoulder at the man in the pink robe. He closed his eyes and took in a deep breath. He reached into his shirt pocket and withdrew a plastic card key.

"Take him to the far side of the campus to North Hall. It has a suite with a kitchen. I'll drop off some food later. All the summer students are staying on the opposite side of campus in East Hall, so he won't be spotted." and Donnatello held the card key out in front of the detective. Derek grabbed it, but it remained firm in Donnatello's hand. "But just as a precaution, I suggest you keep him tucked inside."

"Just think of it as you're saving a man's life."

"If I lose my job because of this," Donnatello warned. "It'll be your life that'll need saving."

Derek snatched the card and shifted the Ferrari into first. "Will never happen," and the black import rumbled forward onto campus. He looked in the rear view mirror to find Donnatello shaking his head.

There were still three police cruisers on the premises as the Ferrari rolled to halt onto the cobblestone driveway. The flashing red and blue lights added to his headache. He opened the door and slowly pried himself from the leather interior. His mid-section was tight. He took a minute to catch his breath as he surveyed his home.

It had been littered with the yellow crime scene tape and he could see the camera flash of the police photographers who were still snapping pictures. Most of the Crime Scene Unit were packing their bags and calling it a night. Only a few remained. He was tired and desperately wanted a chance to sleep. He did not have the energy to answer another barrage of questions. He took in a deep breath and started on his way into the abyss of disorder, which had now made its way onto his doorstep.

At the front door he looked at the police detective who was dusting the security pad on the wall. In the living room he could see the other detectives questioning the models. He found Courtney sitting on the stairway with another plain clothes detective who looked like Bubba Smith from the *Police Academy* movies. She had not caught

his eye, so he re-focused his attention to the detective studying the security system.

"Find anything?" Derek asked.

The detective looked at him with a blank face. He was skinny and wore glasses.

He had on a pair of jeans and his tweed jacket hung loosely upon his shoulders. His

hair was ruffled along with his mustache. After a minute of eyeing the black man in

front of him, the skinny detective went back to the system.

"This is a very intricate system indeed," the police detective responded. "Master

craftsmanship. Who installed this?"

"I don't know," Derek answered. "My father had someone install it."

"Then I'd go back to whoever your father hired and talk to them, because nobody

has tampered with this thing. There's only one set of fingerprints, which I'm assuming

is yours."

"Could there have been a system glitch?"

"Checked for that," answered the skinny man. He was now taking off the latex

gloves. "I took this thing apart and the wires are all in place, in fact they still look

brand new. Are you sure you entered the code?"

"After a certain time, it comes on by itself."

The skinny detective chuckled to himself. He knelt down to his tool chest and

began to pack his utensils. "Then it beats the hell out of me. Your system's fine.

Whoever, got in here, must've been a ghost."

The black detective winced as he sighed. The expansion of his lungs caused him undue pressure to his midsection. He would have to be more considerate next time. He thanked the detective while he formulated his own hypothesis. None of which were plausible.

He stepped further into the house and saw the blood on the foyer. He replayed the night's images in his mind.

"Say goodnight Indigo."

A soft pop echoed throughout the foyer. Derek looked on from the island as he saw Indy's head jerk back. Her arms and legs went limp. He reached the edge of the foyer as Indy's body slowly turned sideways. Derek could see the passion for life leaving Indy's eyes as she fell to the floor.

"Say goodnight Indigo?" he muttered to himself. More questions were filling his mind. If the killer was after Mallott like he presumed, how did they know Indigo? Or were they after Indigo all along? But how could they have gotten into the house without the alarm going off?

Pain suddenly coursed through his body as he felt arms encircle his back. He gritted his teeth as he found Courtney wrapped around him. He pried her away and swallowed hard as he tried to catch his breath. "I'm glad to see you too, but the doctor warned me about excessive hugging of the opposite sex."

"Are you okay?" she asked. "When I saw you being loaded into the ambulance I didn't know what to think. I thought I lost you."

He raised an eyebrow and began crossing the living room towards his bedroom.

Courtney followed. "It'll take a little more than a run in with a speeding car."

"Derek, I'm being serious.," she said as they entered his room. She closed the door behind them. "I was really worried. If anything ever happened to you, I don't know what I would do. You have to believe me."

He turned to face her. "Does that mean that you care for me, more than you let on?"

She smiled. "A woman's gotta have her secrets."

He stepped up to her and looked her in the eyes. The love he felt denied him from restoring the memories of his mother, Sydney's sister Tessa, and E's life-threatening consequence when she attempted to save his life. The love between them would defeat all resistance in accomplishing its goal. He knew what Dr. Gellar had suggested was the right course of action to take. He would not have a second chance. She needed to know how he felt about her. She needed to know that he loved her and he would continue to love her.

He ran the back of his hand across her cheek and then through her long hair. It was soft as silk. His voice was soft and passionate. "No more secrets," and he went to kiss her.

At first, she pulled away, frightened of what was to come. He watched her react to his gesture. He held his hands firmly behind her head, not to be denied. He went to kiss her again. She pulled back, but not in time. Their lips touched. After a moment they slowly broke apart in realization of what happened. Quickly, they searched each other's eyes in hopes they would find something that would sway them from their present course. He could see the defiance in her eyes slip away and she could see the fire in his ignite. Both could feel the emanation of a seed that had been planted a long time ago.

It blossomed when their lips merged again.

His hands slipped down from the back of her neck, caressing her back and encircled her tiny waist. His tongue continued to probe in and out of her wet mouth as a tiny moan escaped her.

At that moment, he pulled away from her searching her eyes again, but they were cloudy with her lust. He felt his saliva mix with hers. It was a sweet taste. In one quick move, he pulled her back close to him and lifted her up cupping her buttocks. She caught her breath as she buried her face into the nook of his neck tasting his skin, placing tiny kisses down his neck. He laid her down on the bed as their lips met once again. This time, with more hunger in their search for each other. They took turns undressing each other and in a matter of moments their naked bodies meshed together with him on top of her.

He knew exactly how to play her. He kissed her body in adoration and his touch was sweet and gentle, but there was urgency behind it. He quelled his thirst as she released a low moan of ecstasy when he plunged into her. He began slow, looking deep in her eyes, never wandering from her gaze. Her legs wrapped around him tight, her bottom slightly lifting in the air. His heart raced. He felt an amazing soul connection that engulfed both their spirits. He moved in her deeper and faster. Her head rolled back on the pillow taking all the pleasure he was giving her.

His name escaped her lips as he began to build to that special feeling. Her fingers grasped his hips. Her blond hair flowed across the pillow as she matched his rhythm. The sound of skin on skin grinding against one another and their soft cries began to fill the room. Together they climaxed; her legs began to shake as he gently hovered above her. He searched her eyes looking for some evidence that she regretted her actions. He could not find any as he listened to their fast breathing.

They laid there for a while, not speaking. He was still inside of her, arms wrapped tightly around her warm naked body. He so much wanted to speak first, but was at a loss for words. So she remained in his arms, his lover at last. It was then he felt the tear fall upon his chest and join in the pool of his sweat, mixing as one. It was a symbolic representation that a part of her and a part of him were once again in harmony.

"I love you." he said with surrender.

A warm breeze accompanied the rising sun as his arms stretched out. His eyes closed as he began channeling his energy. His breathing slowed as he began inhaling through the nose and exhaling through the mouth. He could feel his heart slowing. Slowly his arm extended beginning his morning Kata. His feet began to glide across the sand.

She wrapped the blanket tighter around her naked body as she took a seat on the stair of the wooden deck. She watched him, following his every movement. It looked like a well-practiced dance. The precision of each move and the concentration it took to produce it.

The movements were slow and despite the soreness in his rib cage, it would quickly accelerate. Suddenly, it would stop to resume its slow pace. Since a child, his involvement with the martial arts served as a foundation for his life. He used its discipline to govern his decisions, he used its movements to keep healthy and he used its teachings to grow with each obstacle encountered.

His arms reached out wide as if he was embracing the morning sun. With his Kata concluded, he bowed out of respect. He turned and gave a smile to the spectator on the wooden stair. She was huddled in the blanket from the bed. The steam rising from the coffee mug she was cradling seemed inviting.

"I never told you how much I enjoy watching you do that." she said.

He walked up to the staircase and sat down beside her. He could smell the coffee in the mug. It was warm and sweet. "No, you haven't."

She took a sip of the coffee and offered to share. He took the mug letting the warmth circulate through his hands. He took a sip and handed it back to her. She took another sip watching the sun become a full circle over the horizon. She inhaled deeply and leaned forward resting her elbows on her knees.

"So where do we go from here?" she asked.

He raised an eyebrow. "You tell me," he replied. "Was last night something that you felt, or just a roll in the hay with an old classmate?"

She looked at him. "That sounds a little harsh," she said. "I like to think of last night as something special."

He looked at her, searching for some truth in her brown eyes.

She replied to his silence. "I woke up this morning feeling something I haven't felt for a long time. I often wondered what it would be like when we saw each other again. I will admit that when I left to pursue my modeling career, I was running away. I was scared and in doing so, I ran away from my feelings and the one person who meant more to me than anything else." She smiled at him as she placed the coffee mug on the wooden stair. She then lovingly cupped his hands. "I love you too. I've never stopped loving you."

He swallowed hard and looked out towards the waves that were crashing upon the sand. His nose captured the sea air and he spoke. "There's something I need to tell you."

Courtney leaned backwards in defense. "Oh no," she smiled. "You're gay?"

He let out a chuckle. "I think you know that answer to that question," he spied on a seagull that was circling the beach for its breakfast. It squawked as it swooped downwards. He turned from the seagull, to the Glamour Girl model beside him. "Before you left for California, I was going to ask you to marry me."

Her eyes got wide. She tried to find the words to speak. "Why didn't you?"

"I knew that if I asked you to marry me, you wouldn't go to California. I didn't think I had the right to hold you back from your dreams of becoming a model. So I held off."

Her thumb rubbed the top of his hand. "Can I tell you something?"

He nodded.

They looked longingly into each other's eyes. "Becoming a model wasn't the only dream I had."

He did not know what to say. Everything that was in the past was now coming to the present. They were beginning to pick up the pieces and start from where they left off. Their love went full circle and they recognized it.

She took her hand and placed it on his cheek. Her thumb rubbing the contours of his jaw. "Just exactly what are you trying to say?" he asked.

She smiled as she leaned closer to his face. "I had a chance to grow up," she replied softly. "Who knows? I might like the last name Chase."

He smiled as he leaned forward. Their lips embraced and their tongues danced together in sweet melody as he removed the blanket from her body. Her strong arms encircled his body as he supported her. He allowed his fingers to run through her hair as his other hand caressed her breast. They were firm, but soft to the touch. Her nipples were erect from the gentle morning breeze cascading along the beach.

He pulled her close and led her to the warm sand as they explored their kiss. It was not long before he was upon her and re-summoning the passion they shared the night before. She liberated herself and he could sense the vigor emanating from her soft skin. It was stimulating and vibrant. Their muffled panting was drowned by the

surf tumbling in from the Atlantic. They made love throughout the early morning until

the sun settled slightly below its blue and white backdrop.

<u>**Chapter Nine:**</u>

He picked up the portable phone from its resting place beside the sofa. He sat down and sank within the plush pillows. He dialed a familiar number and hit the speaker button on the charger. He then returned the phone to its station. He winced in slight pain as he stretched for a file on the coffee table in front of him. Though he wore a loose, white Polo and khaki shorts, his mid-section felt restricted. He placed his hands above his head and reached in hopes of stretching the tightness away.

The room bellowed with the ring of the phone as he took in a deep breath expanding his lungs in hopes that a stretch and deep breath would take the soreness away. He opened the file he had brought out from the den. It was the owner's manual for the security system of the beach house. He had hoped that the person who answered the phone would be able to help him decipher how the system could be bypassed without leaving a trace that it was ever tampered with in the first place.

A male voice answered on the third ring.

"Thank you for calling Security Technologies. This is Rick, how may I help you?"

He flipped through the paper work and found his information. "This is Derek Chase, security code Alpha Tango Delta Charlie two…two…nine. The address is six… twenty-two… South Atlantic Avenue. Verify and confirm."

"Please standby," came the voice. After a moment it returned. "Thank you Mr. Chase. Security code and address verified and confirmed. How may I help you today?"

"Did you monitor any lapse in your system last night, around nine o'clock to one?"

"Standby. No, sir. There were no system glitches last night between the times you mentioned."

"I had a break in last night and the security console doesn't seem to have been tampered with. Do you have the ability to view my system's information from last night."

"Yes we do, Mr. Chase, please stand by while I look up that information. I apologize that our system did not live up to your expectations. I will also send out the forms necessary for you to record this incident. Please return this information promptly so that we may better service you in the future."

"Thank you."

"Mr. Chase, I have the information from last night. It seems that the correct access code for 622 South Atlantic Avenue was entered in at approximately 11:10 eastern standard time. Your alarm is self-activated each night at ten P.M., were you out late last night sir?"

"No. I was home all night."

"Have you shared the code with anyone else?"

"No. Only me and my father know the code, and he is currently on a business trip."

"Do you know if he shared the code with anyone else?"

"No I don't, but I do intend to find that out."

"Very well," the customer service representative responded. "It seems very unlikely that someone would be able to guess the code. Our system was designed with state of the art equipment. It cannot be bypassed."

The detective gave a huff. "Well, somebody got past it. There's a chalk outline of a dead woman in my foyer to prove it."

"I apologize Mr. Chase. I was only trying to-

"I understand what you're trying to do," he interrupted. "But that still doesn't help me figure out why the alarm never went off."

"I will have one of our system technicians further investigate. Would that be satisfactory?"

He closed his eyes and nodded. "It would. Thank you."

"You're welcome Mr. Chase. Is there anything else I can do for you today?"

"No. That will be all."

"Very well. Thank you for calling Security Technologies."

Derek disconnected the call and dialed another number. The thought of his father possibly giving the code out to someone else had not crossed his mind. Who would his father know that would want to kill a beautiful model? Where was the connection?

The monotone ringing of the telephone echoed through the living room as he closed the file with the owner's manual. It was a pleasant surprise to hear a familiar soft female voice answering on the fourth ring.

"Hello?"

"Crystal?" He asked. "What are you doing home? I thought you were in Brazil, on a business trip for dad?"

"Hey Derek," his sister relayed. "I was, but things worked out better than I had planned."

"You didn't hurt anybody did you?" he asked with a smile.

He could hear a giggle escape. "No, I just threatened."

"You know people might start to say you're all teeth and no bite."

"They might, but I'm sure the people I *have* bitten will tell them otherwise."

Derek chuckled. "Hmm. Maybe I should use your public relations department?"

Crystal laughed. "Doubt it. What can I do for you my dear brother?"

"Well first of all, you still need to tell me when you're coming down. Master Roo keeps asking about you."

"I'll be down the end of the summer. Tell Master Roo to prepare."

He laughed slightly. Their martial arts instructor teased Crystal about the high amount of energy she possessed, and how well she channeled it. He used her as a way to unlock his own energy. He poured all of his teachings into her, in hopes that one day, she might succeed him as a master.

"I will." He acknowledged. He then gave a smirk. "Is our beloved father home?"

"No he isn't." she responded. He knew she could hear his sarcastic tone. "He's out of town on his own business trip. He won't be home for another two days." She changed the subject to address the sarcasm in her brother's voice. "You know brother dear, he means well."

"The jury is still deliberating that."

"Give him a chance will ya?" she asked. "For me?"

He sighed. His sister had a way about getting what she wanted. She had inherited her mother's charm. Resistance was delusive. "I won't make any promises," he responded. "But I'll try. Tell Dad I called."

"I will," Crystal responded. "What's going on anyway? You only call Dad when there's an emergency."

"Well, it's not really an emergency. Someone broke into the house last night and killed one of the models staying at my house."

"How come the security system didn't work. The beach house has an alarm right?"

"It does, but I think someone bypassed it."

"That's impossible. Nobody is able to bypass that alarm, not even the people who created it. Only way you can bypass it is if you know the code."

"Same thing I was thinking," Derek replied. "I just need to ask Dad if anyone else knew the code."

"Derek, I don't even know the code," Crystal responded. "I seriously doubt someone else does."

"Well, someone knows and I need to find out who."

"Well, I'll tell Dad you called. He'll be interested to hear this."

"I'm sure he will," he added. "You take care of yourself, okay. I love you."

"I love you too; and by the way, I've always known how to take care of myself. You're just too stubborn to believe it."

"Gotta look out for my little sister."

He could hear her sigh. "Always the big brother. Just make sure you take care of yourself, okay?"

"Always. See you soon."

He disconnected the call and sat back in the sofa. With him and Crystal being the youngest, their bond was the strongest. They relied on each other in so many ways. Sometimes it was hard for others to tell who the older sibling was. They were always there and supporting the other in every endeavor.

Courtney stepped out of his room wearing an olive pant suit. Her honey blonde hair was up in a bun and her black handbag matched her shoes. The cream blouse brought out the color in her face. She looked like Olivia Lockehart's protégé, ready to take on the world. She was the only Glamour Girl model allowed to run errands for

Ms. Lockehart. There were rumors amongst the models that she was being groomed to take Olivia's place when she retired.

She walked up and bent over to kiss him on the lips. It was a sweet kiss. The kind that married couples gave each other when they were off to work. "I'll be back late tonight," she said and then she rattled off her list of things to do. "I'm on my way to the Western Union office. Someone needs to notify Indy's parents in St. Croix. After that, I'll be stopping by the photo shoot at Norfolk International Airport to check in with the girls. Lastly, but certainly not least, a few of our financial backers are flying in this evening. Olivia and I will be taking them out to dinner, to discuss the budget for the fall. Don't wait up for me okay?"

"I won't."

"Do you want me to pick you up anything?" she asked rising to her full height.

"No," He replied. "I'll be okay."

"Okay, I'll see you tonight then."

"Hey Courtney," he began. "How well, did you know Indy?"

She cocked her head to the side. "She's been with Glamour Girls for about a year now."

"Did she get along okay with everybody?"

Courtney giggled. "She was a wild one, it was hard *not* to get along with her. She was the one who brought energy to our shows. It's gonna be hard to replace her."

"Were there any lunatics sending her fan mail?"

"We're the hottest thing since the swimsuit edition of Sports Illustrated. Of course we get lunatics sending us fan mail. It wouldn't be show business without it."

"Anything in particular that stuck out in your mind?"

Courtney looked at the ceiling and shook her head. "There was this one guy in Europe, but he had the intelligence of a concrete block. Other than that, I can't think of anybody else. What are you getting at?"

"The intruder knew her Courtney. I distinctly remember hearing him say goodnight Indigo."

"But who could do such a thing, and how did they get in the house?"

"I'm still trying to figure that out; but in the meanwhile, be careful out there. I'm not sure if Indy's the only one. He might be after all of you."

Courtney's voice softened. "Oh my God."

Derek stood up from the couch and wrapped his arms around her. "But I'm not going to let that happen. I promise."

"You better."

"I will. Now you better get going or you're gonna be late."

She kissed him again and he watched her walk out of the front door. His thoughts then returned to the dilemma at hand. How was someone able to input the security code to the alarm system, and more importantly who? He looked at his watch to find that his morning was drawing to a close. His father would not be home for the next two days, so he could not discuss the situation with him. However, he wondered if the people closest to his father could shed some light on the situation.

<u>**Chapter Ten:**</u>

For one o'clock in the afternoon, the FBI's Special Crimes Division seemed unusually quiet. He expected men and women in dark, conservative business attire hustling about in search of a federal infraction. Instead, the office traffic was minimal. A few agents were at their desks typing up reports. He could hear and see the others congregating at the bulletin board, questioning each other on the various memos that were posted. He wondered if there was such a thing as a "special crime" in Virginia Beach, doubting if his tax dollars were being utilized wisely.

He found Special Agent in Charge, Reginald Logan in a glass office. He was sipping on a cup of coffee reading a file. He had not noticed his best friend's son standing outside of the office. In fact, when Derek looked around, none of the federal agents paid much attention to the young black man in khaki shorts and a polo shirt. He could have been a pizza delivery boy, or a man with C4 explosives strapped to his chest. Whichever the case, the earlier notion of his tax dollars going to waste were being confirmed.

He walked up and tapped on the office door. Reggie looked up from his folder and smiled. "Derek!" he greeted as he closed the file. He stood up and walked around the office desk. "What brings you down here?" he asked extending his hand.

Derek shook his hand with a smile. "I need you to answer some questions for me."

Reginald offered a seat. "Of course. What's on your mind?"

The detective smiled and took a seat. His body sank within the leather cushion. "The beach house was broken into last night," he began.

"What about the alarm system your father keeps bragging about?"

"That's exactly what I want to talk to you about. It seems that the alarm system was bypassed. When I talked to the company that created it, they advised that the correct pass code had been entered. But that's impossible, nobody else knows the code except for me and my father."

Reggie sat on the edge of his desk and folded him arms. "Yeah, your father was very anal when it came down to keeping secrets. With everything that was going on within the family business, he couldn't afford not to."

"Would you do me a favor?"

Reggie grinned. "Your father saved my black ass from the Viet Cong back in 'Nam. I could do you a couple of favors."

"I know the FBI has an extensive criminal database. Could you do a search looking for people currently suspected to be in the Virginia Beach area with extensive knowledge of computer hacking and assassination. Eliminate anybody that is shorter than 5'8". You may also want to cross reference them with the travel agencies for recent trips to Europe."

Reggie's eyebrows raised. "Well, that was detailed enough," he said with a smile. "That almost sounded like something I would tell one of these guys to do. Are you bucking for my job?" he joked.

He smiled back at the Special Agent In-Charge. "Not a chance." he then nodded back towards the bulletin board. "You guys have too much free time on your hands."

"Free time?" Reggie remarked sarcastically. He then glanced out through his office window to see what Derek had taken note of earlier. "Oh I see. Just because you see a few agents dawdling around, you think our job is slack do you?" he chuckled quietly. "That's funny," then his tone hardened. "Actually, the office is only half full. We lost contact with one of our undercover agents last week. They were investigating a smuggling ring. When we last talked, we were setting up a meet to turn the evidence over and arrest the whole organization. But nothing ever works out the way it's planned. I suspect, that our agent is dead. I have people scouring the city for leads."

"Well, I wish you the best of luck, but I have a case of my own to unravel."

"Derek, if somebody broke into your house and knew the code, you better be on your guard. Your father had many enemies by the time he left South America. They may try to get to you to get to him. Be careful."

"Always."

Reggie stood up from the desk and extended his hand. "You know, you may want to talk to Slappy, he might be able to help. He and your father were close too."

Derek shook his surrogate uncle's hand. "I was planning on it. Thanks Reggie."

"Don't mention it."

"Bypassed the security system?" Slappy asked as he removed the apron from his patron's chest. Loose hair floated carelessly to the tiled floor. "You're shittin' me? Someone used the pass code that only your father knows, went into the house and shot one of the models dead?"

"Right in front of me."

"Are you okay?" Slappy asked looking past Derek's shoulder at the crowd of patrons waiting for a haircut. He looked back at his previous customer who was fishing in his wallet. He mouthed thank you when the customer extended his hand with a wad full of money.

Derek nodded. "It's disturbing to know that someone else knows how to get into my home."

"Be careful, someone may be coming after you to get to your father."

"That's what Reggie said, but I don't think I was the target."

"How you figure?"

"Before the model was shot, the guy addressed her by name."

Slappy spun the chair around and shooed the small traces of hair off the red leather barber chair. "So he knew her huh?"

"Looks that way. I have Reggie gathering some information for me."

"Well, watch your back. Your father has some powerful enemies."

Derek took in a deep breath. "I've been thinking about that. Ever since my father moved the headquarters from Columbia to the United States, I've been concerned that the Elders of San Puliero are going to retaliate."

"Out of respect of your grandfather, they probably won't, but I would have my doubts about Diego Tosillio. He was the original choice as a replacement for your grandfather's organization. From what I've heard, he's one ruthless sonovabitch."

"You suspect Diego?"

"No doubt in my ex-military mind. Honestly, I think he was behind your mother's death."

"You know they say my mother's death was an accident?"

"Yeah, but you and I know differently." Slappy said as he sat down in the barber's chair. He folded the apron across his lap. "Your mother's death being an accident is about as true as a woman with three tits. What about the accident report from the Navy? The one that mentions the broken tail-lights? Or the extra set of skid marks? I still believe she was forced off the road and it was covered up."

"Someone on the inside maybe?"

"Maybe? It would explain a lot of things. It might even explain who knew the access code to your beach house."

Derek took in a deep breath and his objectivity returned. "It is something to think about, but unless Diego is staking claim to the fashion world, I don't believe it was one of his minions last night. Nonetheless, I'll watch my back."

"When Diego is concerned, you betta watch your back, your front and everywhere in between!"

"I hear ya, but if Diego does decide to come into my backyard, he'll have to deal with me, not my father."

Slappy chuckled as he shook his head realizing that Derek would smirk at his next statement. "I know. You are nothing like your father. He's a lot meaner."

It was uncommon for Norfolk International Airport to have its distant sounds of screeching tires of planes landing drowned out by the loud Latin flavor of Ricky Martin's "La Vida Loca". Even as the powerful engine of the Ferrari idled, he could hear the upbeat tempo of the music take control of its environment. He had parked a few feet from a rented Leer Jet, which served as the backdrop for the Glamour Girls' photo session. He looked at the model standing by the private jet, recognizing her as the one who sprayed him with the squirt gun the day before. He remembered her name to be Alexis.

Her smile was playful as she teased the camera and the small crowd of off-duty airport personnel. He ceased the engine, watching her spin around in her red two-piece evening gown. Its halter top exposed her toned abdomen and the strings in the back keeping the material together, left her back naked. He smiled as she lifted her long hair to expose her shoulders. He could see the photographer fighting to get as many pictures as he could from each angle.

Standing beside the photographer and the mostly male populated crowd of bystanders, was Courtney looking on with eyes of a director. He could tell she was searching her mind for the best pose. Her decisions would no doubt be a factor in determining if she would succeed Olivia Lockehart.

He stepped out of the Ferrari and started towards the photo shoot. He was still asking himself questions as to how someone could break into his home without the alarm going off. He was also bothered by the fact that someone knew their target well enough to address them by name. It could only lead to someone within Glamour Girls, but who could that be? And how could they learn the access code to the beach house. He hoped Reggie's search would have something that he could use to make sense of all the loose ends.

He was within a couple of steps of Courtney and the photographer when he saw a small dark image against the fiberglass hull of the Leer Jet. He concentrated on the image until he made out a figure. It was holding what looked like to be a rifle. He quickly yelled "Get down!" as he sprinted towards the model, but his warning was drowned out by the photo shoot's loud music.

He grunted when he pushed one of the few spectators out of his way. His duty to protect Alexis, as well as the other models at the photo shoot, was never more critical than this moment. He leapt onto the small platform and dove towards Alexis. He tackled her onto the ground just as a loud shot echoed over the music. He could hear the shot ricochet harmlessly off the hull of the Leer jet. It almost blended in with the sound of those in attendance as they screamed and dove to the ground realizing the gravity of the situation.

Alexis's coughing confirmed that she was no worse for wear than getting the wind knocked out of her. He quickly glanced towards the origin of the sharpshooter to find the dark figure slinging the rifle over his shoulder and relaying a two finger salute before running off behind a baggage carrier.

Derek gritted his teeth as he and Alexis rose to their feet. He would have to wait until another opportunity presented itself to pursue the would-be assassin. With the immediate danger deferred, the crew of Glamour Girls Inc. quickly ran up to assess the situation. Courtney was in front of them all leading the charge.

"Are you okay?" he asked.

Alexis looked around as her breathing became more stable. "Yeah, I think so."

"What was that?" Courtney asked.

Derek nodded and pointed to the now vacant area where the sniper waited. "A sniper. He was over near the baggage area."

Courtney looked over at her production assistants and addressed them all together. "Call the cops! Tell them what happened and to get their asses over here ASAP!" He lifted his eyebrows. He hadn't seen this side of Courtney before. She was demanding and in full control as she assessed the situation and exercised her authority. "Are you okay sweetie?" Her caring nature was stepping in.

Alexis nodded. She then looked down at her dress, it was ripped along the sides exposing her thighs. "This outfit has seen better days though."

Courtney smiled. "Don't worry about it. I'm sure it'll compliment the designer's intentions anyway." She looked around and then addressed the group. "We're gonna call it a wrap for today, but don't pack anything up. I'm sure the police are gonna want to examine the area and question everybody that was here." She then looked back at Alexis. "Why don't you go back to the trailer and change, we'll take care of everything here."

Her bottom lip was trembling when Alexis said. "I'm sorry Courtney."

Courtney put her arms around and kissed her on the forehead. "Don't be. I'm just glad you're still with us."

He watched as Courtney sent the Glamour Girl model away. The look of purpose refilled her face. "Are you okay?" He asked.

She was angry and frustrated. "No!" She snapped back. "I almost lost another friend. First it was Indy, and now this!"

He stepped up and placed his arms around her. He squeezed her gently hoping it would comfort her. She succumbed to his gesture for a moment before she stepped away. He knew she was protecting her image as Olivia Lockehart's protégé. He respected that. He also respected her decision to call the cops. It would be a futile gesture because he was sure the sniper left no traces of his self. "It's probably a good thing to call the cops, but I can tell you right now they're not going to find anything."

"Why is that?" She asked.

Derek took in a deep breath hoping his news would not frighten the girls any more than what they were, but his gut knew otherwise. There were other concerns beginning to surface in his mind. "This was a warning shot."

"What the hell do you mean a warning shot? He almost killed Alexis up there."

Derek shook his head in disagreement. "When I realized what was happening, it still took me a little time to get to Alexis. If he wanted her dead, he had enough time to do it."

"Maybe he wasn't completely set up?"

"Maybe. If it is the same person that broke into my house and killed Indy, he's a pro. Pro's don't usually have poor set ups. They're usually very detailed oriented. Their target area is scoped out weeks in advance and they have a daily diary of their target, or targets in this case. The guy we're dealing with knows everything about Glamour Girls." Derek quickly remembered the two finger salute. It was like the sniper was introducing himself. "He also knows everything about me."

"So what does that mean?"

"It means we're up to our necks in trouble. We gotta find this guy and fast, or the next picture anybody takes of us will have a chalk outline around it."

<u>**Chapter Eleven:**</u>

The phone rang as Derek sat in front of the computer terminal. He was downloading the files that Reggie sent. There were six matches fitting his requested search parameters. It would be another moment before he could look at the potential faces of his would-be assassin.

"This is Chase."

"You paged me?" Saundra asked on the other line.

"Yes, I did. I need you to do me a favor."

"What kind of favor?"

He thought for a moment about what he was going to say. Just in case the person who was able to break into his house was also able to tap his phone, he had to be cautious. He was still responsible for Mallott and despite his suspicions that Indigo's murder was unrelated, he did not want to compromise Mallott's current situation any further.

"I need you to go to campus. I left a present for you."

"You left me a present?" Saundra sounded surprised. "But why?"

"Just think of it as my way of saying how special you are."

"Ahh, that's so sweet."

"Just ask the security guard where I put it, okay."

"Can I go get it now?"

"Sure, just call me on my cell phone when you get it okay?"

"Okay. Thank you Derek, you're so sweet."

"Don't mention it."

She hung up the phone and Derek smiled knowing that when Saundra called him back, she would be upset that he lied to her. At least on the cell phone, he could talk to her without the fear of being bugged. He could give her instructions and keep a watchful eye on Mallott while he figured out the issue with Glamour Girls and their unknown stalker.

His computer beeped, acknowledging the completion of the file download. "Okay." He said aloud to himself. "Who is our first contestant?"

There was a knock on the door frame as he double clicked on the first downloaded file. He turned towards the door to find the remaining models of Glamour Girls peeking around the corner. He smiled at the sight of five women fighting to catch a glimpse of what he was doing. He immediately recognized Alexis, but had not met the other four. He nodded for them to come in and returned his gaze upon the screen.

"Mr. Chase," Alexis asked. "Is it true?"

"Is what true?"

A mocha colored woman stepped past Alexis. Her voice was sweet and almost motherly. "What Courtney said about somebody trying to kill us?"

Derek took in a deep breath contemplating how he wanted to answer that question. His notion of Mallott being the assassin's target was slowly being dismissed. As far as he suspected, whoever was stalking the models, was potentially stalking him as well. "I'm still trying to figure that out."

"Is there anything we can do to help?" asked the slender oriental model. Her hair had been tied into a bun and her pink halter top creased against the door frame as she waited for her colleagues to enter the den.

Derek smiled. "Yes, there is." He could sense the girls' eagerness as they hurried up beside him and the computer. "A friend from the FBI sent me some files of suspected assassins in the area. Maybe you ladies can take a look and see if you recognize anybody."

They looked at the first man on the computer screen. His unshaven face was haggard underneath the mug shot case number. His dark hair was ruffled and the mole on the side of his neck looked ominous.

"He looks like somebody Tasha would date." Alexis started with a giggle.

Derek turned towards the model Alexis was talking to. She was a buxom redhead sporting black sweatpants and a Boston Red Sox T-shirt. She looked over at Alexis and smirked.

"At least I date men."

Derek's eyebrows raised realizing too much information had been divulged. Ignoring the beginnings of a verbal cat-fight, he looked back at the screen and quickly read the file for himself. It seemed that the first suspect was currently working at a youth center and assisting the activities director with extra-curricular events. He read a little further to discover that the suspect was doing his duties confined to a wheelchair. He had been injured in a car crash six months ago.

With the click of a button the file was closed and another file was opened. Cat calls were quickly whistled by the girls as the face of their second suspect appeared. His blonde hair made a nice accessory to surfing playboy image. Even with the mug shot photo, he seemed like he was posing. Derek theorized that if this potential killer had chosen another line of work, he could have been on the cover of GQ or some surfing magazine.

"He's a hottie!" said the oriental model.

The mocha colored model giggled as she addressed her oriental counterpart with a hi-five. "You got that right Mei Ling."

Mei Ling reciprocated the hi-five and they slapped hands. "Makes you want to tie him up and lick him all the way down, doesn't it Valerie?"

"Like a lollipop."

Derek shook his head amazed at the conversation they were having. It almost sounded like the same conversations he had within his male circle of friends. He reminded himself of Courtney's taunting and devilish smile during the photo-shoot on his balcony, the incident in the driveway with Alexis and Indigo, and Indigo's stimulating striptease before being shot dead in the middle of his foyer. He solidified his belief that Glamour Girls Incorporated had an insatiable thirst for pushing the envelope in every endeavor.

"Ladies," he said. "I don't mean to sound like a bore, but may I remind you that one of these men may be trying to kill you."

The giggling stopped as Alexis spoke up trying to hide her smile. "Sorry." She apologized. She then cleared her throat and looked at the computer screen. "No, we haven't seen that guy before."

He clicked on another file and the picture of a bald black man with a goatee filled the screen. According to the information in the file, the bald man was a former Marine turned mercenary.

"That looks like your brother Valerie," one of the models retorted. She had short black hair with a face full of soft curves. Derek assumed that her name was Brooke, the only model who had not partaken in any of the previous conversations.

"Yeah, it kinda does, but my brother died four years ago doing stunt work."

Derek read more of the information in the file to find that this suspect's whereabouts were unknown and could possibly be in the Virginia Beach area. The detective made a mental note of the information, etching the suspect's name, Raymond Jarvis Jr., and the suspect's face into his memory.

"Do any of you recognize this man?"

"No," Tasha replied as the others shook their head in agreement. "He doesn't look familiar."

Derek rubbed the stubble of his goatee as another face appeared on the screen. The girls shook their heads. He scanned the information to find that suspect number four was currently under close surveillance by the FBI with detailed accounts of the suspect's transactions. None of which could be intercepted by Derek. He came across the same information for suspect number five.

He opened the last downloaded file and a woman's face appeared on the monitor. The detective blinked his eyes as he perused the information below her picture. Her name was Michelle Gomez and she was a Cuban refugee who enlisted in the Marine Corp as soon as she was old enough to salute. Further reading disclosed that she was a weapons expert with sniper training. Her whereabouts were unknown, but suspected to be in the Virginia Beach area. Was she the one pulling the trigger at the photo shoot in Norfolk? Why the hesitation? From what he knew of snipers and from his conversations with Sydney, who was a trained sniper herself, the decision to execute the kill shot was quick. It was something that required split second timing. There was no hesitation or the opportunity would be lost. His confusion grew when he started asking himself how Michelle Gomez could be related to Indigo's murder?

His answer came when Brooke uttered. "Holy shit."

"What?" Derek asked.

"That's Indy's sister!"

The detective looked at the screen to see if he could see the resemblance. After a moment, he could pick out a few similarities with her eyes and her jaw line, but this woman was older by at least six years. "I thought Indy was from St. Croix."

"Not originally." Alexis replied.

Valerie chimed in behind her. "Her parents are originally from Cuba. They escaped to Miami where they stayed for years illegally."

"Yeah," Mei Ling said. "Nobody caught on until Indy was well into college. Her sister had already joined the Marine Corp and Indy had found some way to get her green card, so her parents moved to St. Croix."

"Indy talked about her sister all the time." Tasha said. "She had all these pictures of her sister in uniform during the Gulf War and shit like that."

"After a while," Brooke interjected. "It became a bore."

"I can't believe her sister is trying to kill us." Alexis said.

Derek shook his head as he looked at Michelle Gomez's employment history. "Don't go jumping to conclusions. What's her motive? Why would she want to kill her sister and the rest of you?"

"Cause we're beautiful and she's not?" Tasha answered.

Derek held back his sarcastic chuckle. Confidence was definitely a Glamour Girl's strength as well as her short-coming. "I doubt that would be her reason, but we'll keep that option available. Jealously could very well have a hand in it."

"Why would anybody want to kill us?" Brooke asked.

His mind re-processed the information as he re-read Michelle Gomez's employment history. Her last job was with Griffin Securities. He was quickly blind-sided by feelings from the past like a wide-receiver leaping in the air for that touchdown pass only to be hammered out of bounds before his feet could land in the end zone. Despite his personal objections, he had another lead to follow.

"I'm not sure," he responded answering Brooke's question. "But I know somebody who might be able to point me in the right direction."

The amusement on the face of Thomas Janocky III disturbed him. It was as if Janocky expected to see him eventually. The former proprietor of Griffin Securities sat at a wooden table handcuffed to its sides. The orange prison garb enhanced the former business man's black hair, which seemed to harbor more gray streaks than what the detective had remembered. Janocky's medium build had filled the orange jumpsuit with an essence of muscle tone. The prison guard stood by the door and nodded politely as Derek took a seat at the other end of the table.

The southern drawl was crisp and inviting. "Good day Mr. Chase. To what do I owe the pleasure?"

Derek was instantly reminded of the annoyance Janocky's voice caused his ears. "I need some information."

"Isn't that just a pig's ass?" Janocky retorted. "You want me to give you information after what you did to me? What's the matter? Too many dead ends trying to find out who murdered your mother?"

The annoyance was igniting the fuse to the black detective's anger. He knew Janocky had information regarding his mother's death. What it was and how he knew it bothered him. Though Janocky had many connections within law enforcement and military agencies, Derek could not fathom why the information regarding his mother would be so valuable. However, he placed his past in the back of his head. His visit had another agenda that needed to be fulfilled.

"This isn't about my mother. It's about Michelle Gomez."

"What about her?"

"You tell me. She used to work for Griffin Securities."

Janocky laughed. "I have another month before my trial which I'm sure my lawyers will be victorious. After all, I do have friends in high places. And when I do get out of this piss smelling hell hole, I am going to make your life worth shit. Tell you about Michelle Gomez? I'd just assume you kiss my ass."

He leaned back in his chair and shook his head with a chuckle. "You know Janocky, you're not the only one with friends in high places. You've been here for about a month now, right? I'm sure you've heard of Johnny Spence?"

"Yeah, what of him?"

Derek smiled as he played his trump card. "When I was a rookie cop, my partner and I just happened to be in the right place at the right time. I saved his sister from being shot to death during a drive-by. When he came to pick her up from the station, I helped him fill out the paperwork and recommended some counselors that worked with victims of violent crimes. It's unfortunate that he's in here for killing those poor bastards that tried to kill his sister, but I hear he's doing well on the inside and that he kinda runs things. I also hear he can make people disappear on the inside, no questions asked. I truly would hate for you to miss your trial all because I had to collect on a favor."

"My word," came the southern drawl. "Are you blackmailing me Mr. Chase?"

"Not at all," Derek smiled. "Just offering you an option." He leaned forward and smiled politely. "Let me ask you again. Tell me about Michelle Gomez!"

Janocky stared at the detective who seemed to be searing with anger and frustration, but hiding it with kindness. It was a good tactic. "Michelle Gomez?"

"Don't play games with me Janocky. I'm not a patient man today."

Janocky's eyes went towards the ceiling as he recalled the information. "Ah yes, Michelle Gomez. She was with Griffin Securities for a short time before pursuing her own reckless endeavors." He almost sounded fatherly as he continued speaking. "She had a lot of potential."

"Potential for what?"

"To be the best counter-intelligence operative this nation has ever seen. Unfortunately, she had no discipline which eventually got her and her boyfriend kicked out of the Marine Corp and subsequently fired from my employ."

"She had a boyfriend?"

"Why yes. Big bald black man. I believe his name was Jarvis. Ray Jarvis."

Derek raised an eyebrow. His situation had just gotten more complicated. Instead of dealing with one potential assassin, he had to contend with the possibility of two potential assassins. "If I wanted to find her, where would she be?"

"It's hard to say." Janocky answered. "She never stays in one place and she only worked for me part-time. She and her boyfriend are like soldiers of fortune, so they were usually out of the country on some covert mission, usually somewhere in South America."

The detective's tone became demanding. "Think again."

Janocky fidgeted in his chair. "You could try Apollo's Gym off of Princess Anne. She likes to work out. If she's in the country, that's where she'll be."

Derek folded his arms. "What about her boyfriend?"

The former businessman shrugged. "There's not much I can tell you. Seen him once or twice. He's a big some bitch, and he doesn't speak much. I doubt he's even in the country."

He processed the information and looked at his watch. It was close to six o'clock. He looked over at Janocky and his objective switched gears. It was time to address his past.

"What do you know about my mother's death?"

A smile slowly went across Janocky's face. "What's it worth to you?"

Derek looked at him and then stood from the chair. "Forget it."

Janocky tried to reach out and motion for him to stay, but the handcuffs clinked against the restraints of the table. "No Mr. Chase, don't go."

The detective looked at the man in the orange jumpsuit. "Talk."

Janocky took in a deep breath. "Let me preface this by saying that the information I'm about to give you is classified. This is bigger than you can imagine. There is a hydra of powerful people involved. People I used to work with when I was in the service during Vietnam."

There was surprise in Derek's voice. "You were in the service?"

"I was an intelligence officer, covert ops."

"I'm getting impatient Janocky. What does this have to do with my mother?"

The prisoner lifted his hand up in defense. "I don't know his name, but I do know he was in love with her. So much in love that he convinced her to have an affair."

"What!?"

Janocky quickly continued with purpose. "She would go to a cottage high up in the mountain of La Cabra on the outskirts of San Puliero. The cottage was the meeting place. On the day of your mother's accident she went there to break off the affair."

His heart thumped hard against his chest. He still could not believe what he was hearing. "You're lying you sonovabitch!"

"Am I?" Janocky asked. His southern drawl was echoing through the room. "I'm sorry to taint that angelic image of your mother, but face it Mr. Chase. Your mother was a tramp. The man who killed her was the same person she had an affair with."

Derek yelled as he lunged towards Janocky. He was stopped short by the prison guard who had been observing the situation. Janocky laughed as Derek struggled to get free from the guard's hold. Unable to break the hold, Derek took a moment and calmed himself. He straightened his shirt and pointed at Janocky.

"I should've killed you when I had the chance."

Janocky smiled as he relaxed in his seat. "Don't blame me. I'm only the messenger."

"How do you know all of this?"

"I worked for Navy intelligence. My job was to maintain surveillance in the area.
I knew about your father, your grandfather and the role they played in San Puliero. So
it was only natural for me to know about your mother's extramarital activities."

"Then who was she having an affair with?"

"Honestly Mr. Chase, I don't know. The man she was having an affair with
would leave the cottage wearing a hat. It was tilted over his face just enough to prevent
clear identification. It was like he knew we were watching."

"Did your surveillance see who forced my mother off the road?"

"No." Janocky answered. "Because the accident was so close to the military
base, the Navy sent a team to investigate. I presented my findings, but was met with
interference from the town's police department and the CIA. Eventually, the report
was squashed."

Derek seemed intrigued as the guard released him, but stood close by. "Wait a
minute. You wrote the forensics report for the Navy?"

Janocky nodded. "Despite what you think of me, I could be an asset to your
investigation. As I said before, I know a lot of people in high places."

Derek was quiet for a moment. Though Janocky's information was helpful, he
would not compromise his integrity. He quickly dismissed the idea of a partnership.
"You said the CIA was interfering with the investigation. Why?"

"I don't know, but they were always two steps behind me. They took the
evidence we gathered and the report once our investigation was complete." Janocky

sighed realizing the investigator had ignored his suggestion. "Mr. Chase, I have told

you all that I can. May I suggest you talk to your father? I'm sure he knows the truth."

<u>**Chapter Twelve**</u>:

The warm breeze caressed his nose as he hid behind one of the marble statues his grandfather imported from Italy. *He watched his mother gather the white roses into the wicker basket as she picked them from the garden. She quietly hummed as she went through the covered nursery. He strained his ears and smiled recognizing her humming as something he fell asleep to.*

"You've been standing behind that statue for ten minutes now." She said without looking at him. " You don't have to hide," she continued as she clipped the base to another rose. "You can help me if you want."

He stepped from the statue and slowly walked up to his mother.

She looked at him and smiled. She handed him the basket of flowers. "Would you carry this for me?"

He nodded as he took hold of the basket. "Mommy? When will I meet Michael?"

His mother rubbed the sides of her stomach. Her pregnancy would soon come to an end. "It should be any day now."

"Will I like him?"

His mother smiled and laughed softly. "I sure hope so."

"Will he like me?"

His mother caressed his face. "You will be his big brother. I'm sure he will. After all, you are Crystal's big brother and I know she just adores you."

"But Crystal is a girl, and she doesn't like to play in the mud after it rains."

His mother laughed. "You shouldn't like to play in the mud either."

"Allyson plays in the mud after it rains."

"Hmm," his mother responded. "Is that so?"

Their conversation was interrupted with the distant sounds of protest. His mother looked towards the patio entrance to the house. Allyson quickly appeared. She was laughing and had a camera in her hand. She stopped and looked at her mother and her younger brother.

"Is that Victoria's camera?" his mother asked.

"Yes," Allyson answered. "She read my diary, so I'm borrowing her camera." She aimed the camera at the two of them. "Say cheese."

His mother pulled him close as she straightened her posture. They smiled as the flash illuminated the nursery. The distant sounds of protest grew louder as Allyson giggled. "Thanks mom!"

His mother shook her head as Allyson ran off disappearing back inside the house. A moment later, Victoria stepped into the patio's doorway. The look on her face was not a pleasant one as she panted.

"Mom? Have you seen Allyson? She has my camera."

"As a matter of fact, she just took our picture," his mother replied. "Did you read her diary?"

Victoria took in a deep breath and sighed. "Yes, but it was an accident. I thought it was mine."

His mother smiled, restraining herself from giggling. "Tell Allyson, that you're sorry and that I want her to give you back your camera. Just make sure that the next time you're paying attention to whose name is on the diary. Understood?"

"Yes, mother," Victoria surrendered before disappearing within the house after her sister.

His mother took in a deep breath and looked down at him. "Can you believe we'll have another addition to our family?"

He looked at her and she smiled at him. Her fingers stroked through his hair as he looked at her. His mother was beautiful. He smiled back, but then realized that his mother's face had suddenly turned pale.

"Oh my," she said calmly to herself as she looked down towards the ground. "That was unexpected."

He looked down at the ground searching for what she was looking at. He then looked up to find a spot growing on the front of her khaki maternity shorts. She slowly eased herself to the ground and motioned for him to run into the house.

"Sweetheart, go get your father. I think Michael is coming."

He took one final look at the picture of him and his mother in the garden before placing it back on the bookshelf. He stood looking out the window watching the waves crash against the beach. He missed his mother terribly, and to hear rumors that she had an affair, from a man who made his living on deception, was unsettling to him.

Arms suddenly encircled his body as a familiar scent entered his nostrils. "You miss her don't you?"

He turned as Courtney's hug became tighter. He returned the embrace. "Yes."

There was a hint of wine in her kiss. The taste was sweet and inviting as she pressed up against him. Their lips parted, but she still remained close to his face. "She will always be with you. You know that right?"

"Yes."

"Then don't worry about it," she said. "You'll find out what happened."

He took in a deep breath and reflected on her words. She was right. He would find the truth one day. He cleared his throat and pushed his memories aside to focus on the love in his arms. "How was the rest of your day?"

She smiled when she answered. "Well, let's see. After the incident at the airport, I spent the rest of the afternoon talking with police detectives and making sure Olivia didn't postpone the remaining photo shoots. She and I then had dinner with our financial backers."

"Well, I guess that explains the metallic briefcase sitting in the corner." He spoke. He noticed it instantly because it seemed like an odd fixture amongst the den's decor.

She looked back over her shoulder and found what he was looking at. The thin metallic briefcase sat next to his bulletproof vest and his gun. "Oh yeah," she scoffed.

"It's full of money." She returned her gaze on him and kissed him full on the lips, her tongue probing his mouth.

"It must've have been a good meeting." He mumbled as they kissed.

"Better than I imagined," she mumbled back. Her kiss became hungrier. "I know it's almost 8:30, but whadaya say we call it a night?"

His cell phone rang interrupting the notion of another passion filled night. He squeezed her tightly before breaking away. "Sorry," he said reaching for the cell phone. "I'm on the clock."

She frowned as she accepted his excuse. She took a step backwards and quietly mouthed. "I want you."

"This is Chase." He answered as he shook his head. He read her lips that were pleading with him to reconsider. He watched her as she tried to tempt him with a seductive dance.

"A present for me huh?" Saundra's voice boomed. "I don't consider being a babysitter for a man in a pink robe a present."

"No." He silently said to Courtney. She gave a frown and a humpf before flopping down onto the den's leather couch. "I'm sorry Saundra, but I needed your help. My house was broken into last night and one of the models was shot dead. The man in the pink robe is a material witness for the U.S. District Attorney's office. I needed a safe place to put him. I can't be there with him because I'm trying to find out exactly what the hell is going on."

"So why all the cloak and dagger stuff?"

“Just covering my ass.”

“So when do I stop playing nurse maid?”

Derek chuckled. “In a couple of days. How’s he doing?”

“Besides being a few snaps away from getting his butt whooped, he’s doing fine.”

He had an idea of the trouble Mallott was getting into. “Is he drooling?”

“I can’t seem to stay three feet away from him. He’s a horn-dog. It’s like he missed college or something.”

Derek chuckled again. He knew Saundra could easily defend herself against Mallott. His quest would end up with him biting off more than he could chew. Derek sighed. “I’ll be there later tonight to check on him. I have a lead to follow up on.”

“You better make it quick.” Saundra warned. “You wouldn’t want the eleven o’clock news to have this late breaking story that a man in a pink robe mysteriously died with a foot up his butt on a college campus.”

“I’ll see what I can do.”

He disconnected the call and took in a deep breath preparing himself for more investigative work. He looked over at Courtney who was slowly unbuttoning her cream colored blouse.

“Are you sure you don’t wanna stay?” she gestured opening her shirt. She was offering herself and her breast sat in the white bra waiting for his response. It was an enticing offer. “I’m going to be busy with work all day tomorrow. A girl like me could use some T-L-C.”

He walked up and kissed her. “No can do. I need to go to the gym.”

Her devilish smile appeared. "Why go to the gym, when I can make you sweat here?"

His eyebrows raised. "I'm not looking for that type of work-out." He smiled. "Besides, I just had a shower."

"I can give you a good reason to take another."

He chuckled. "Maybe next time." He kissed her again and started for the door. "Don't stay up too late."

She scowled and fell back into the plush leather of the couch. "I don't have a reason to anymore."

He blew her a kiss. "Believe me Miss Lathaye. When this is all over, you and I will have forever."

"Promise?"

He held up his two fingers. "Scout's honor."

Courtney smirked. "But you were never a scout."

It was Derek's turn to smile devilishly as he walked out of the den.

Saliva's "Click Click Boom" reverberated throughout Apollo's Gym drowning out the clanking of metal slapping against metal. He scanned the gym noticing that there were only a few patrons working out. One woman was on the treadmill, while the rest worked out with free weights. He looked over at the front desk to find it vacant. He would have to find Michelle Gomez by interrupting someone's exercise.

He walked over towards two men bench pressing what looked like the entire rack of weights. The man lifting the weights looked as if he had won a few strongman competitions and was setting his sights on the world championship. His suntanned body was lifting the weights with ease. Though the veins in his neck mapped a course from shoulder to head, he was calmly exhaling after every lift. His spotter was just as built but had a spiked hairdo and the absence of a neck. Both ignored the detective's presence, maintaining their focus on the barbell.

"How many pounds is that?" Derek asked.

"Three hundred." The spotter answered.

Derek whistled. Three hundred was impressive. *He could easily throw my ass across the room.*

The clang of the heavy metal echoed throughout the gym as the weight lifter concluded his workout. "Can we help you with something?" He asked.

Derek gave a nod. "I'm looking for Michelle Gomez."

"Never heard of her." The spotter answered.

"Sorry man." The weight lifter apologized.

The detective stood there un-wavered. "Funny. Someone extremely close to her said she's always here when she's not off fighting some war with her boyfriend."

"Told you man," the weight lifter said standing up from the bench. "Don't know the lady. Even if we did, why you lookin' for her?"

"That's between me and Michelle."

"Like we said before," the spotter added. "Haven't seen her."

Derek smiled as he shook his head. He watched the weight lifter turn and look at his exercise partner with dissatisfaction. In this instance, the stereotype was proven true. There was brawn, but the brains were lacking. "Just a minute ago, you said you didn't know her. Now you haven't seen her? Which is it boys?"

The weight lifter scowled when his gaze returned to Derek. "What my colleague here is trying to say is that we don't take kindly to strangers looking for our friends."

Derek could feel the adrenaline building in his body. "So she's a friend of yours? Why didn't you just say that in the beginning?"

"Because I don't like you."

He took in a deep breath as his hand curled up into a ball. "Then you really aren't going to like this."

Derek recoiled and quickly sent a punch to the weight-lifter's jaw. The head snapped back, but the target stood unmoving. The weight lifter smiled as he reached for the detective. He lifted Derek into the air and threw him a couple of yards away.

The black investigator landed sideways against an exercise bike. He silently swore to himself for picking the fight. He turned as the spotter with no neck ran up to him. Derek quickly found a free weight in the rack beside the exercise bike. He grabbed one of the weights and flung it like a Frisbee towards his attacker. It caught the spotter in the breadbasket, stopping him in his tracks and doubling him over. Derek quickly stood to his feet and grabbed a five pound dumbbell. He used the free weight

to send an uppercut, lifting the spotter into the air, and onto his back unmoving.

He could feel a foot kicking the free weight out of his hand. He turned only to

get a jaw full of knuckles. The force of the blow sent him rolling sideways across the

floor. He quickly scrambled to his feet as his jaw throbbed. He looked up to find his

attacker charging. Decidedly, he retreated further within the gym with the weight lifter

in close pursuit. He stopped once he returned to the bench where the weight lifter was

bench pressing the three hundred pounds.

"Listen, don't make me hurt you." Derek warned. "Just tell me where Michelle

is and I'll be on my way."

The weight lifter charged and Derek hopped on the bench and slid underneath the

barbell. The weight lifter lunged for him as the detective released the pin holding the

arms of the bench press in position. The weight lifter spun onto his back as three

hundred pounds of free weights came down. The attacker caught the weight before it

crushed his chest.

Derek found himself in the spotter position as the weight lifter went to lift the

three hundred pounds. The detective grabbed the bar. He then took in a deep breath

and used his weight to press the barbell down upon the weight lifter's chest.

"Whew," Derek began. "That looks heavy." He commented allowing some of

the weight to be taken off as he withdrew from pressing down upon the barbell. "Let

me help you with that."

The weight lifter grunted as he started to bench press the barbell. "Man, I'm gonna fuck you up!"

Derek shook his head as he shifted his weight back upon the barbell. It quickly sank into the man's chest. "Nah. I don't think so."

The weight lifter squirmed as he fought to lift the weight. Despites his efforts, it stayed firmly in place. Derek did what he could to apply more pressure. He heard a moan coming from the other weight lifter that had been unconscious from his kiss with the free weight. He was slow in getting up.

"Where's Michelle Gomez?"

"Go to hell!" the weight lifter struggled to say.

"Wrong answer." Derek retorted as his foot found leverage against the mirrored wall. His full body weight was now adding to the three hundred pound weight. "I won't ask again. Where's Michelle Gomez?"

The weight lifter sucked in a big breath of air. "Why?"

Derek sighed. "If you must know. It's about her sister."

"What about her sister?" asked a voice from the corner.

The detective looked up to find Ray Jarvis staring him down with a 9mm Berretta. He was wearing camouflaged pants and an army green T-shirt. He looked like a stunt double from the A-Team. Derek removed his feet from the mirror and onto the floor, rising to his normal height. The barbell crashed onto the floor as the weight lifter coughed for air.

"You won't need that." Derek responded.

"What do you know about her sister?"

"She's dead."

He cocked the gun. "You're lying."

Derek raised his hands. "She and the other models were staying at my beach house last night. Someone broke in and shot her."

The weight lifter caught his breath and growled as he stood up. He looked at the detective like he was about to charge. He stopped as a shot rang out.

"Stand down soldier!" Jarvis ordered. He re-cocked the weapon and aimed it back at Derek. "Are you a cop?"

"No." Derek answered. "Just someone trying to find answers."

"To what kind of questions?"

"Who would want to kill her sister and why?"

Jarvis uncocked the pistol and tucked it in the front of his pants. "Beats the hell out of me. Indy was always in some type of trouble."

"When was the last time Michelle talked with her sister?"

Jarvis shrugged and scratched his bald head. "Uh, I say the last time they talked was sometime last week when Indy was still in Europe."

"Do you know if they made plans to meet each other while Indy was in Virginia Beach?"

"That I don't know. Indy had told her sister that she would be extremely busy seeing how this would be her last job and all."

The detective raised an eyebrow. "What do you mean last job? She was getting out of the modeling business?"

Jarvis rubbed the coarse goatee on his chin. "Shit!" he began. "Indigo was so much more than just a model."

Derek motioned for him to continue, but stopped as he heard a click from the back room where Jarvis had been hiding. It sounded like a weapon being cocked, specifically like a machine gun being primed to fire. Jarvis must have heard the sound also, because he was withdrawing the Beretta and turning to find where the noise came from.

Derek looked past Jarvis's shoulder to find the muzzle of an M-16 peeking around the corner. He quickly dove onto the floor as the barrel of the M-16 spun towards Jarvis. What happened next seemed to play in slow motion.

The M-16 started chugging out rounds of bullets as the patrons of Apollo's Gym ducked for cover. Derek quickly slithered across the floor in search of a column, desk, anything that would protect him from the automatic rifle's fury. He glanced to find one masked assailant in black garb making his way into the gym. It looked like the sniper from the Glamour Girl photo shoot at the airport. Derek figured that the assassin had managed to quickly sneak in through the back door.

He crawled behind the vacant desk as he heard Jarvis cry out. He peered over the counter to find the soldier of fortune firing his weapon as bullets peppered his chest. He witnessed Jarvis stumbling backwards and crashing against the mirrored glass.

The weight lifter with the spiked hair charged the attacker with the assault rifle and placed him in a bear hug. The attacker quickly sent the back of his head against the bridge of the weight lifter's nose sending him backwards teary eyed causing the body builder to release the black garbed assassin. The gunman turned and unleashed the full fury of the weapon on the weight lifter. The bullets lifted the spiked haired, muscle man slightly into the air and sent him crashing down into a treadmill.

Derek quickly ducked down as the firing stopped. He could hear the ejection of the magazine cartridge of the assault rifle. His hand quickly reached for the gun in the small of his back. *Shit!* He left it at home! His heart thumped wildly as he listened to a fresh magazine being loaded and primed in the military assault rifle. His absentmindedness would cost him his life. He had to think quickly.

But how the hell could he have forgotten his gun? When he was on the clock he always carried a weapon, if not two. He took in a deep breath quickly chastising himself and suddenly realized he wasn't wearing his bullet proof vest. *Shit!* Why was he so unfocused? What had changed?

The answer hit him just as the front door crashed open. He looked over to find E storming inside with a couple of uniformed officers. The masked assailant trained his weapon on the newcomers and fired. He watched as E and the other officers ducked for cover. They returned fire, forcing the assassin to retreat to the back room. Sirens echoed in the background as E motioned for the two uniform officers to take pursuit. Weapons trained on the doorway leading to the back room, they slowly followed after the gunman.

E re-holstered her weapon, as the sounds of police back up grew louder. She walked over to the detective. "Are you okay?"

He glanced around the corner to find Raymond Jarvis slumped down on the floor still clutching the 9mm Beretta. His cold dead eyes stared back at the detective. "Not sure." He said returning his gaze to the female officer. "I'm not sure."

<u>**Chapter Thirteen**</u>:

"Why is it that every time I have a homicide in Virginia Beach, you're not far behind?"

Derek took in a deep breath as Austin bellowed his dissatisfaction with the situation. He had not moved from behind the desk. He reflected on the distraction that permitted him to walk into a situation unprepared. Had he not been preoccupied with Courtney, maybe he would have remembered to carry his weapon, or to put on the bulletproof vest.

But how could it have been her fault? He asked himself. She only wanted to be with him. *And I want to be with her.* He confirmed. *I just need to focus. From this point on, when I'm working, no more distractions.*

"Chase?" Austin echoed. "Are you listening to me?"

"Yes," Derek said getting to his feet. He mocked the Lt.'s voice. "Why am I always involved in your homicide cases?"

"Well?"

Derek shrugged. "Maybe, by some strange twist of fate, you and I are supposed to become friends?"

"I'm not in the mood Chase." Austin smirked. "When you and I become friends, Hell will be having a sale on ice skates."

"Then it's probably a good thing I don't skate."

The police Lieutenant growled as he withdrew a notepad from his police windbreaker. "Raymond Jarvis," Austin began. "Some type of soldier of fortune on the FBI's most wanted listed. Only one known associate, his girlfriend, Michelle Gomez, who is also on the FBI's most wanted." Austin then turned to Derek. The Lieutenant's look was stern. "Her known associates include a mother and father in St. Croix and a sister, who's naked body just happens to be in my morgue. How you got all this information is beyond me, but I thought I told you to let us handle this?"

The private investigator looked around as the crime scene unit scoured the work out facility with their brushes and rubber gloves. He looked back at the Lt. and sighed. "Austin, you couldn't handle this if you tried."

"Oh yeah?" The Lieutenant challenged. "How so?"

Derek waved his hand around the area as E walked up. "Look at this place. This is the work of one man with an M-16. He hit this place hard and fast."

"He also disappeared without a trace." E added. "We've set up a five mile grid with two aerial units in a sweeping pattern."

Austin rubbed his forehead. "Okay. Keep me posted."

E gave a glance at Derek, which he took as a heed to be careful, before returning to the mish mosh of uniform officers and SWAT personnel. Derek took one last look at Ray Jarvis. Photographers and crime scene officers were huddled around the body

searching for clues. He took in a deep breath as a thought entered his mind.

"I don't think Jarvis was the only target." He said as he started to exit Apollo's

Gym. Austin looked at him curiously. He could hear the anticipation in Derek's voice.

"I think this guy was after me as well."

"Then maybe I should get out of his way!" The police Lt. shouted back at the

investigator as he opened the glass door to the gym. He watched as the detective

walked a short distance across the parking lot to his car. He raised an eyebrow

contemplating Derek's statement. His eyes followed the detective as he got into the

Ferrari and drove off into the night.

**The dark campus of Virginia Wesleyan College was a calm alternative to the

shattered debris of Apollo's Gym.** He piloted the Ferrari down the paved path

towards the guardhouse hoping Donnatello was on duty. Explaining his circumstances

as to why he needed to be on campus after hours to one of the other security guards

would present a compromising predicament.

He breathed a sigh of relief recognizing Donnatello's Mustang sitting within an

orange coned perimeter. He flipped the lights off as he rolled to a stop. He could see

Donnatello's chagrin as he greeted the import.

"Tell me you're here to pick up that walking disaster."

Derek smiled as he shook his head.

Donnatello started relaying his story. "Ever since you dropped off the Energizer Bunny, he has been calling me every single night, every hour on the hour. He wants to know if I could order him some pizza, get him some magazines, and stuff like that. I told him if he didn't leave me the hell alone, I would -

"I'm sorry Donnie."

The security guard's face changed from anger to confusion. "Sorry? Do you know I can get fired for this if someone finds out?"

Derek held up his hands in defense. "Yes, I know; and I appreciate everything that you're doing. There's a student here by the name of Saundra Wilkins. She is an intern for Garrett and Taylor, and she is gonna stay with him for a couple of days to make sure he stays out of trouble."

Donnatello glanced at the phone in the guardhouse. Derek observed the bewilderment on his face. "I wondered why he hadn't called me yet."

"Look," Derek continued. "Two more days, that's all I ask."

Donnatello took in a deep breath. "Two days?"

"Two days."

The security guard looked upwards as if he was pleading for a way to disappear. His cheeks puffed out as he gave in. However, he turned to Derek with a stern face. "If I get fired over this -

Derek chuckled. "Donnie, it'll never come down to you getting fired. I'll make sure of it."

Donnatello gave a smirk before returning to the confines of the guardhouse. "You better."

The detective shifted the car into first chuckling. "When's your break?"

"In fifteen minutes."

"Cool. When you go on your break, meet me over there." Derek said as the Ferrari rolled forward.

Donnatello gave a nod as he returned to his duties. Derek eased the Ferrari onto campus and started for Mallott's temporary safe house. Interpreting the recollection of the last couple of days, Virginia Wesleyan was shielded from the misadventures that seemed to follow him. Donnatello's job would stay intact.

"When can I blow this joint?" Mallott asked as he gulped a can of soda. "This place is cramping my style."

Saundra gasped in disagreement. "What style?"

Mallott's head whirled towards Saundra. "Don't let the pink robe fool you. I am a connoisseur of fine quality."

"You worked at a hardware store." Derek said. "What do you know about quality?"

Mallott looked at the detective with amazement. "First off, hardware stores are all about quality. Secondly, the hardware store I worked for was also owned by Tony Cooke, who's a retired mobster from New York who thinks he's Bob Villa with Al Capone's cash. Trust me. If I know anything, it's quality."

Saundra smirked. "You may know quality," she said nodding at the pink robe. "But your taste leaves something to be desired."

Mallott looked at the robe and then back at Saundra as if he was a dog that had been put outside for the night for having an accident in the family room. "This is cashmere! Mrs. Cooke gave this to me for Christmas."

Saundra cocked her head to the side. "That would be one gift that would go back to Santa."

Derek chuckled as he interrupted their exchange. "You say Mrs. Cooke gave that to you for Christmas? Why?"

Mallott shrugged. "I don't know."

Derek could hear the uncertainty in Mallott's voice. He often heard that tone coming from people with something to hide. What was Mallott hiding? He shook his head as he leaned against the wall. "C'mon fess up." He said. "What the real reason why Tony Cooke wants you out of the way?" He stood for a moment and then lowered his head in regards to what he was going to say next. He could detect the exasperation in his voice. "Tell me you didn't have a thing with Mrs. Cooke."

Mallott held up his hands defensively. "She's leaving the guy! He treats her like crap!" The federal witness then slouched back into his seat. "And she loves me."

Derek sighed. "She loves you? How can you be for sure?"

Mallott shrugged. "I just am. She loves me."

The detective shook his head as Saundra chimed in. "Well, they say love is blind."

Mallott gave a scowl. "Joke all you want, but just as soon as we can, we're gonna get married and run away to some place warm with a name I can't pronounce."

"Only if Tony Cooke doesn't kill the both of you first."

"He won't have the chance." Mallott boasted. "My testimony is gonna put him in jail for a very long time. By the time he gets out, we won't even know who we are."

"We'll see." Derek replied.

Saundra leaned back in the chair. "Do you think Cooke knows about you and his wife?"

Mallott shrugged. "Nah. He's too busy with his business to even pay attention to her."

"Are you sure?" Derek asked.

"Of course I'm sure." Mallott replied.

Derek folded his arms. "You'd be surprised. Sometimes a person may look stupid just so they can observe everything."

"I'm telling you, the man doesn't know anything. He's oblivious!"

"We'll see."

"So if Mrs. Cooke is so unhappy," Saundra began. "Why doesn't she just leave him?"

"It's not that easy. Cooke gives her everything."

"And she's leaving him for you?" Derek asked. "C'mon Mallott, somethin' doesn't add up."

"Trust me," Mallott replied. "Love endures all. You can ask her yourself. She should be here any minute."

"What?" Derek yelled as he pushed himself from the wall. His booming question caused both Mallott and Saundra to jump. "What the hell do you mean she'll be here any minute?"

Mallott tried to crawl into his skin afraid to speak. He swallowed hard before speaking. "I called her to let her know that I was alright. She said she wanted to see me."

Derek looked upwards as if he was asking for deliverance. He then took in a deep breath and stared at the federal witness. "I can't believe the risk you're willing to take."

"What risk?" Mallott asked. "Who's she gonna tell?"

"Who knows?" Derek answered. "She may blab to the whole city or she may not say anything at all. Fact of the matter is, you are a federal witness in protective custody, my protective custody. That means, you don't talk to anybody unless I say so. Otherwise, you're dead. If you're dead, then you're no good to anybody, including Mrs. Cooke if she truly loves you."

A knock on the door distracted Mallott from replying. Derek motioned for him to hide as he approached the room's heavy wooden door. "Who is it?" Derek asked.

"Open the door." Donnatello's voice echoed. "It's me."

Derek twisted the knob and swung the door open. His eyes went wide when he recognized the two large, handsomely dressed men from the Ramada standing in front of him. He recalled that their encounter at the hotel had ended with one of the well-dressed hockey player look-alikes taking a swim in the outdoor pool and the other picking himself up from the concrete patio. This encounter would be in their favor.

His heart thumped wildly against his chest as one of Tony Cooke's men held, who he assumed, was Mrs. Cooke over his shoulder like a sack of potatoes. She was kicking frantically, with her high heels flailing about like a wounded animal and protesting in a high pitch whine. Her captor stood there ignorant of her plea. He smiled as he ran his fingers through his long black hair.

Derek looked over at the other henchman, who was wearing a tweed jacket. The movements of his jaw seemed mechanical as a wise-ass grin began to display his satisfaction. He was slightly taller than his long-haired partner, but just as stocky. His hefty left hand was gripping the back of Donnatello's neck and his massive right hand seemed to swallow the pistol pointing at Derek's chest.

The private investigator looked at Donnatello with disappointment. "I'm sorry to get you involved in all of this Donnie."

Even with the stranglehold around the back of his neck, Donnatello's complacent attitude persevered. "I appreciate the apology, but as soon as this is over, I'm gonna kick your - "

The college campus security guard quickly spun around grabbing the wrist of his captor as Derek sent a foot towards the gun kicking it out of the massive hand. The henchman holding Tony Cooke's wife threw her legs over his shoulder sending her towards the ground with a soft thud and a yelp. He charged towards Derek.

Derek focused his attention from Donnatello, who now had forced his captor to his knees, to the attacking henchman. The private investigator growled as he responded with a jump front kick. He could feel the attacker's head quickly snap backwards as his foot connected with his aggressor's chin. The assailant stumbled backwards before finally crashing against the wall and falling face first onto the dormitory floor unconscious. He looked back at Donnatello who had sent a fist across his captor's jaw knocking him out. The security guard cursed as he grabbed his knuckles in pain.

"You okay?" Derek asked.

Donnatello shook some feeling back into his hand. "I think I just punched a brick wall."

Derek chuckled. "It just proves what Master Roo always says."

"Yeah," Donnatello replied. "The bigger they are, the harder you have to hit."

Mallott ran past the two and knelt over the woman who had been abruptly tossed onto the ground. "You okay, Doll-face?"

She nodded as she slowly rose to her feet. "Oh Walty."

"Walty?" Saundra spoke out.

Mallott ignored the intern from Garrett and Taylor and continued his focus on Mrs. Cooke's well-being. "They didn't hurt you, did they Doll-face?"

She shook her head. "No." She answered scampering over to the unconscious thug who dropped her onto the floor. She sent one of her high-heeled shoes into his rib cage. "You big oaf."

Derek took in a deep breath as Donnatello withdrew a pair of zip-ties. The security guard used it to bind the wrists of the two henchmen. "You guys need to get out here." Donnatello started. "I'll clean things up."

"Where can we go?" Mrs. Cooke asked. She was a curly blonde roughly in her late twenties, early thirties. She looked like an actress who took the wrong part in a movie and was fighting to get her career back on track. Her face was heavily painted with red lipstick and pink blush. The blue eye-shadow accented her blue eyes, further exaggerating the look of an out of work actress auditioning for a part in a movie. "I'm sure Tony had these goons follow me here."

The private investigator reviewed his options and replied. "Then I suggest we go to the last place Tony Cooke would look to find you, and it's a place where I know you two won't get into trouble."

<u>**Chapter Fourteen**</u>:

It was well past business hours when Derek knocked on the side door of Buzz Cutts. He could hear music coming from inside. It was loud enough that he easily recognized it as a hip-hop version of "Stand By Me". He knocked again. He knew that Slappy was the last to leave Buzz Cutts in order to tend to his duties as proprietor. His daily tasks would include cleaning the barber shop, random testing of someone's equipment, a call to his other locations for a daily status check, and, if necessary, he would review paperwork and allocate funds for salaries and operational cost.

The door swung open to reveal a welcoming, but confused Slappy. "This mus' be important if you're bringin' white folk into da ghetto at night."

Derek ushered Mallott and Mrs. Cooke inside the side-door entrance of the barbershop. "I need a place for these two love birds to crash for the night."

Slappy raised an eyebrow as Derek checked the scenery one last time before stepping inside. Their presence in the urban neighborhood went unnoticed. "I believe the sign out front says 'Buzz Cutts', not 'Roll In The Hay Motel'."

He smiled at the barber. "C'mon Slappy, it's just for the night. I'll find them some new digs tomorrow."

The owner of Buzz Cutts sighed. He finally motioned for them towards the leather couch burrowed deep within the employee break room. "The couch folds out, go on ahead and get some shut eye."

"Thanks Slappy."

Slappy turned to the detective. "You're gonna owe me big for 'dis one."

Derek nodded. "Yes, I will." He took one last glance at Mallott and Mrs. Cooke who were making their way over to the couch. She clung to the star witness with a genuine smile on her face. Maybe Saundra was right, love was blind.

"And don't think I'm waiting to collect next year." Slappy continued.

His attention diverted back over to the barbershop owner. "Slappy, can I talk to you in private for a moment."

Slappy's bewildered face also displayed a look of concern. He steered the detective over to a corner that was out of earshot from his new tenants. "Sure, what's on your mind?"

Derek took in a deep breath as his mind replayed the latter part of his conversation with Janocky. "How well, did you know my mother?"

Slappy smiled. "I knew her very well. Why?"

"Do you think she was capable of having an affair?"

Slappy looked like someone had just cut out his heart. "Who the hell told you that?"

Derek gave a sigh of regret and silently chastised himself for tainting his mother's memory. "Somebody killed a model in my beach house last night and in the process of trying to find out who, I came across this information."

Slappy scowled. "You still didn't tell me who? I wanna knock some sense in them."

"You don't think it's true?"

"Do you think it's true?" Slappy asked back. Derek stood silent which seemed to irritate the barber even more. "Maybe I oughta slap some sense into you too!" Slappy retorted. "You're mother loved your father and damn anybody else who thinks otherwise!"

"Do you think I like hearing this shit?" Derek began. "But I have to pursue every lead, no matter how it stinks."

Slappy huffed and he brooded. "It stinks to high heaven. I can't believe you would be foolish enough to believe your mother was having an affair."

"I don't believe it either," Derek answered. "But I need to make sure. My mother would want her name cleared."

"Your mother would slap you cross-eyed if she heard you talking this nonsense."

"Slappy," Derek pleaded. "Just help me get this straight in my head and I'll drop it, never to bring it up again."

Slappy's brooding ceased as he sighed. "Your head shouldn't be mixed up in the first place."

Derek took in a deep breath and forced his objectivity to come forth. "Slappy, you were there the day she died. Was she acting strange?"

"No." Slappy answered. "I saw her that morning, before Reggie and I went to town. She was sweet as ever, just humming as she picked flowers. Your father told us she did that each morning so there would be fresh flowers on the breakfast table."

"From what I was told by my father, she was coming from her sister's house."

"Yeah, that's what your father said."

"And they found my mother's wreckage in the mountains near La Cabra?"

"Yeah, what's your point?"

He shrugged. "My mother only had one sister and she lives in the valley. There's no reason why my mother should have been near La Cabra."

Slappy's brooding returned. "You can't seriously be thinking your mother was having an affair?"

Derek sighed as the pit in his stomach grew tighter. He could feel the urge to cry, but held it in check. "Slappy, right now, I don't know what I'm thinking. Why would she be near La Cabra?"

Slappy stood there silently.

He swallowed hard and tried to calm the thumping of his heart against his chest. His mind was drawing conclusions that he did not like. "What if the information is true?"

"It's not true," Slappy defended. "The only thing up there in La Cabra are military installations. I don't know why your mother was up there, but it was not to have an affair! And I just assume we bring this conversation to an end. You gettin' me all worked up again."

"I'm sorry Slappy," Derek apologized. "But affair or not, somebody else was up there at La Cabra. Even though it was omitted from San Puliero's police report, the broken taillights and second set of tire tracks proves that someone killed my mother and my little brother. I won't rest until I find out who."

He yawned as Sydney's fingers danced across the keyboard. The day's events had worn on him physically and mentally, but he fought the fatigue and continued to concentrate on the task at hand, finding out who was responsible for his mother's death.

"Did I mention how much I appreciate you doing this?"

Sydney smiled faintly. "At least twice within the last two minutes."

He reciprocated the smile. "I just know how much trouble you can get into."

With a wave of her hand, she discarded his concern. "Don't worry about it. I didn't realize my departure from the Navy would inspire a few high ranking officials to offer me favors." she giggled. "I should have left sooner." The screen flickered as she finished typing. "Here we go. La Cabra, a U.S. military installation in South America."

"Is there anything special about it?"

"Not really," Sydney answered. "Currently, it's abandoned. According to the file, it was built immediately after the Vietnam War. It was a ten acre compound primarily set up as an alternate base of operations for the military's war against the cartels of the drug trade. There was a compliment of three hundred Marine and Coast Guard personnel on site. It also housed operatives from the various branches of law enforcement, mainly CIA, FBI and DEA."

"Can you pull up personnel files?"

She nodded after a few keystrokes. "Anybody in particular?"

He played a hunch. "Try Michelle Gomez."

He looked over her shoulder as she typed away. After a moment, a military file appeared on the screen. "Major Michelle Marie Gomez, United States Marine Corp." Sydney began. "She is a 1991 graduate of UCLA with a Bachelor in Computer Science. Family lives in St. Croix. It says she was stationed at La Cabra between August 15th, 1992 through September 28th, 2000 before being dishonorably discharged."

"Dishonorably discharged? Does it say why?"

Sydney leaned closer to the screen and read off the information. "Major Gomez's fitness reports and evaluations seem flawless until late August of 2000. There was an incident with one of the local villages. According to a FBI report, a suspected drug trafficker, named Diego Tosillio was moving a large shipment of cocaine to the states. The DEA saw their opportunity to put an end to Tosillio's operation, and they sent Gomez and her team in. However, the report was a farce and Gomez's team walked into a trap. Her entire team was wiped out and the circumstances surrounding her survival were suspicious. She was investigated and later found guilty of conspiring against the United States. She was court martialed with a dishonorable discharge and sentenced to life in prison. She was placed in the brig on the base until she could be transported to the States, but somehow she managed to escape."

"Tough bitch." Derek replied.

Sydney smirked. He could see her Navy pride getting the best of her. "Not really." She said. "There was an insider. His name was-

"Ray Jarvis?" Derek calmly interrupted.

Sydney turned to him. "Yeah, how did you know?"

"I met him earlier tonight," he answered. "when he was still alive."

Sydney stared at him before returning her gaze back to the computer screen. "Well, Jarvis happened to be on watch the night Gomez escaped. Base commanders couldn't prove it, but the report speculates that he is the one who let her go free. A month later, he was dishonorably discharged for insubordination and assaulting an officer."

"Besides family members, does Gomez have any other known associates listed?"

Her fingers tickled a few buttons on the keypad and brought up another screen. "Just one, a Thomas Janocky III." She paused for a moment. "Why does that name sound so familiar?"

"He was the man who conspired to have your sister killed." Derek answered.

Sydney took in a deep breath. "This gets better with each moment." He could tell she was holding her emotions at bay. Being reminded of her sister's death must have been like pouring salt on an open wound. She closed her eyes briefly before continuing to type. "He was her commanding officer at La Cabra."

"Yeah," Derek confirmed. "He was Navy Intelligence at La Cabra." His eyebrows furrowed. "I'm curious. Can you pull up his file?"

She was already typing in the information. After a moment his file appeared on the screen . "Colonel Thomas Janocky III. Stationed at La Cabra as Special Advisor of military operations. A Vietnam veteran highly proficient in jungle warfare and urban combat with a list of commendations and medals, including a Purple Heart. He retired from the military shortly after Gomez escaped."

Sydney used the mouse and clicked on a screen. She gave a low whistle before speaking up. "During Vietnam, Janocky served with Special Forces as a Lieutenant Colonel. His unit specialized in scouting missions. Their primary objective was the infiltration and elimination of enemy base camps."

Derek could feel his body growing more tired. "So?"

"Well, their missions would have gone on unnoticed until they crossed paths with another recon unit establishing a base of operations in an abandoned enemy base camp. Janocky's unit attacked the base camp unaware that they were attacking friendlies."

"What happened?"

"Janocky realized the mistaken identity and averted a catastrophe, but there were a few casualties."

"I don't understand what this has to do with La Cabra?"

Sydney continued. "It took two days for both recon teams to establish a base of operations at the enemy base camp. Then according to the report, they were attacked by an enemy battalion. They were out gunned and outnumbered. During the firefight, the commander of the other recon unit ordered an immediate retreat, but Janocky and his team stayed, fully determined to engage the enemy. They would have been wiped out if the commander of the other recon unit didn't go back for them. It's because of him that Janocky is still alive today."

Derek shrugged. "I'm assuming you have a point to all of this?"

Sydney smiled as she revealed her information. "Wanna know who the commander was of the other recon team?"

"Who?" Derek asked getting impatient. The fatigue was battling back with a vengeance.

"Major Thomas Washington, your father."

At first, he thought he was sleeping when she relayed the information to him. He looked at her as she nodded with confirmation. "My father saved Janocky's life during Vietnam?"

"Yes." Sydney answered. "Received a Medal of Valor for it."

Derek raised an eyebrow as he fought back the urge to sleep. "Can you pull up a roster of Janocky's unit?" He asked remembering a story he heard.

She nodded, and within a few keyboard strokes and mouse clicks, the information appeared on the screen. Derek looked over her shoulder and studied the names on the roster. He recognized two of them.

His eyes opened slowly as the aroma of coffee percolated through Sydney's townhome. Since moving to Virginia Beach, her task of finding a home came quite easily. She found a renovated townhome on the outskirts of what the local affectionately referred to as Chick's Beach. A residential beachfront overlooking the Chesapeake Bay and the twenty-six mile bridge connecting Hampton Roads with the Eastern Shore. Though she had not completely unpacked, her home felt warm and inviting as did the scent of French Vanilla flavored coffee that filled his nose. He looked up to find Sydney sitting across from him. She was already dressed in a dark grey business suit and her dark hair was tied back into a bun. She crossed her legs and took a sip of her coffee as she read the morning paper. His body instinctively stretched as he lifted his face from the plush pillows of her chenille couch.

"Good morning." She said taking another sip of coffee as she continued to read the paper. "Pleasant dreams I take it?"

He smiled. "Your couch is almost as comfortable as mine."

She looked up from the newspaper with a grin. "May I offer you a cup of coffee?"

"No." He answered. "That won't be necessary."

"You were so hell-bent on getting some answers, it took everything I had to get you to stay here last night. You looked exhausted."

He took in a deep breath of air and took in the smell of her living room. The apple smell of the air freshener was somewhat refreshing to his senses. "I apologize for being so stubborn. It's a terrible trait that I share with my father."

"Don't worry about it. I can be the same way." She smiled and placed the newspaper on the table. "After all, part of my job is to take care of my employees."

"Then please accept my gratitude."

She gave a nod as an acceptance.

He stood up with a stretch and something from the newspaper caught his eye. He chuckled when he picked the paper up and read the title out loud. "Rare diamonds from Scotland catches museum's eye."

"What's so amusing?"

He quickly perused the article before answering. "Just thinking back to a conversation I had with Dr. Gellar."

"About the diamonds?"

He smiled. "Yes." He sat down continuing to scan through the article. "About ten million dollars in African diamonds were stolen from an armored car in Paris. If I was a betting man, I'd say Scotland Yard believes the perpetrators are in the US and they are setting a trap." He raised his eyebrows upon further reading. "It looks like a rare set of priceless diamonds will be delivered to Virginia Beach's Museum of Antiquities today at 4pm."

"You think the perpetrators are in Virginia Beach?"

"Or a city nearby. I'm sure Scotland Yard's finest are hot on the trail. "

Sydney shook her head. "You're just a wealth of information."

"I dabble in this or that from time to time."

Sydney took another sip of her coffee. "The more I learn about you, the stranger it gets."

He smiled.

Sydney placed her coffee mug on the table and sat back in her chair. Her demeanor became professional. "How is Mallott?"

Derek smiled sheepishly as he shook his head. "The less you know, the better."

Sydney chuckled. "I thought this would be a walk in the park."

"Nothing is a walk in the park."

"Well, I have good news. The U.S. Marshals should be at the office later on this afternoon to pick him up. The U.S. Attorney moved the trial up a couple of days early. "

Derek nodded. "I will gift wrap him personally."

"Good." Sydney responded as she again changed gears. Her professional tone changed to one of concern. "By the way, I'm glad I could help you last night. I know how important it is for you to find the truth about your mother."

"Yes." He replied. "Thank you very much."

"So what are you going to do now?"

He took in a deep breath. "First, I'm going to go home and take a shower. Then

I'm going to pick up Mallott and have a chat with an old friend."

<u>**Chapter Fifteen**</u>:

Derek had just finished buttoning his shirt as the doorbell rang. He hurriedly tucked the black cotton fabric into his jeans and reached for the Glock sitting on the bed next to a note left by Courtney. She and the other models were doing a photo shoot at Norfolk's Botanical Gardens and would be back that evening. It brought a smile to his face when he read the part about the models treating him to dinner at a fancy restaurant and then afterwards, Courtney would be his dessert. The doorbell rang again as he quickly released the clip from the Glock and checked to make sure it was full. He reloaded the Glock as he started for the door.

He relaxed as he opened the door, but it was short lived when he recognized his guest. The FBI agent that Derek considered a family member stood in the doorway with a smile on his face. The detective stood deciding his next move. The questions he had diminished his level of trust for his father's best friend.

"Aren't you going to invite me in?"

The black investigator raised an eyebrow not quite sure what he should do. He quickly smiled and allowed Reginald Logan into his home. "Sure."

Reginald smiled as he walked inside. "You okay?"

Derek nodded as he closed the door. "Yes. Just need a chance to catch up on some sleep."

Reginald nodded in agreement. "Tell me about it. This missing agent has got us working some long nights at the bureau."

"Still no leads?"

"None," Reginald answered. "They were working undercover in an international smuggling ring. When they contacted us last, they were in Scotland and mentioned something about African diamonds."

Derek raised an eyebrow. "It sounds like you're after the same people Scotland Yard is after."

"Yes. We are working with 'The Yard'." Reginald confirmed. "But there has been no communication from our agent. We fear they were compromised and murdered. But there's no body. It's like they vanished into thin air." He then placed his hands in his pockets. "But a missing field agent is not the reason why I came over."

Derek folded his arms and leaned against the wall. "Really? What's up Uncle Reggie?"

"I wanted to talk to you about your mother."

How convenient. "You have new information?"

Reginald shook his head. "It's not new information, but it is something I think you should be aware of."

"What is it?"

He could hear regret in the FBI agent's sigh. "I can't help but feel responsible for her death, but you're gonna find out sooner or later."

"Find out what?"

"Your father is going to kill me when he finds out that I told you."

"Told me what?"

Reginald was silent for a moment before he spoke. "On the day your mother died, she and I had an argument."

"About what?"

"Her affair with Slappy."

Derek could feel his fist tightening. The betrayal he suddenly felt was becoming fuel for his anger. "Her affair with who? Slappy?"

The FBI agent chastised himself for disclosing the information. "I knew I shouldn't have said anything. This is opening very old wounds."

Derek took a moment before commenting. "The wounds were never healed in the first place."

"I'm sorry Derek," Reginald said. "But you're the son of a man I owe my very life to. I need to put things right."

Derek closed his eyes in hopes his objectivity would re-surface. Most of it stayed burrowed in the base of his stomach, but a little allowed him to continue listening to Reginald's sordid tale. "What happened?"

Reginald rubbed his chin and then sighed. "As you already know, your father invited Slappy and I down the week before your mother died. Slappy was completely infatuated with your mother, and who wouldn't be? She was absolutely magnificent.

Well, one night I went out for a walk, and happened to find them in the greenhouse in

a..." Reginald paused for a minute to choose his words carefully. "um –

compromising situation."

"How did my father find out?"

"Shit." Reginald confessed. "I told him that night! He confronted your mother

and they argued until that morning."

Derek raised his eyebrows in confusion. "I remember seeing Slappy the day my

mother died. He and dad seemed okay."

"That was all of your mother's doing. She told your father that it was she that

seduced Slappy and made your father swear that no matter what, they would remain

friends."

"My father believed this?"

"Not at first, but he loved your mother so much, he granted her wish anyway."

The private investigator stood there absorbing the information. His objectivity

was slowly gaining momentum. "Tell me what you know about Thomas Janocky III."

A puzzled expression went across Reginald's face. "He was my commanding

officer in 'Nam. What does he have to do with all of this?"

"He's currently serving time for corporate espionage and conspiracy to commit

murder. Coincidently, he happened to be at La Cabra when my mother was murdered

and seems to know a lot about her death and the person who killed her."

"La Cabra." Reginald said quietly to himself. He seemed focused on trying to piece a puzzle together within his mind. "I know its home to a military base, but I can't fathom how it's connected? I also don't know how Thomas Janocky III would know about your mother."

Derek moved from the wall and starting pacing slowly. "According to Janocky, he believes the person who killed my mother was the same person she had an affair with."

"That's preposterous!" Reginald acknowledged. "Slappy may have been a louse for seducing your mother, but he's no killer!"

He stopped and gave a scathing look to the FBI agent. "Then who killed her Uncle Reggie?"

Reginald held up his hands in protest. "I don't know, but I'll kill the bastard when I find out. Your mother was a beautiful person inside and out. The whole damn thing is a shame."

"Do you know Michelle Gomez or Ray Jarvis?"

Reginald shook his head. "Who are they?"

"They were at La Cabra. Janocky was also their commanding officer. The people at La Cabra tried to take down Diego Tosillio and a sting led by Gomez was compromised. Gomez survived, was sent to the brig for treason and with Jarvis's help, she escaped. Jarvis was killed last night in a gun fight. She is a freelance mercenary and she's out there somewhere."

"I thought you needed that file to investigate that model that was shot in your house? How is this connected with your mother's death?"

Derek shrugged as he answered. "I'm not sure how it plays into the death of my mother." He looked at Reginald with conviction. "At least not yet."

Reginald read the expression correctly. "What are you getting at? You must be crazy if you think we had anything to do with your mother's death. I have half a mind to come over there and slap your ass."

His tone was slightly apologetic but still demanding. "It doesn't make sense."

"When does it?" answered the FBI agent. "Look, I have always been there for you in the past, let me be there for you now."

He looked at Reginald and refolded his arms.

"Listen Derek," Reginald started. "You have to find out the truth on your own. I understand that. But if you ask me, it's too much of a coincidence that whatever you're working on now has ties with your mother's death. When we heard the news of your mother's death, I went up the mountain with the local police, and Slappy went to tell your father."

Slappy took in a deep breath and lowered his head. "Tom, we heard some talk in the town about Kara. I'm afraid there's been an accident."

His father's knees almost gave way as he stumbled towards the door frame. He clutched his heart. "Oh my God."

"I remember that day." Derek said.

"Yeah. It was a sad day for all of us."

His father turned to find his son in the door frame. He took in a deep breath and went over to his son and knelt down. "Your father is very sad."

"Is it because of mommy?"

His father nodded. "Mommy is taking a little trip right now."

"Is she coming back?"

His father shook his head. He could sense the pain his father was going through and it scared him. "Not now, but one day, we'll see her again. I promise."

"Tom," Slappy started. "We gotta go."

Reginald took in a deep breath snapping Derek into the present. "That's one of the reasons why your father built this beach house. He wanted to make sure one of your mother's dreams came true. I remember the first time I came here, he was so proud of this place. He couldn't wait to show me everything. I must've walked through this house for two hours before I had a chance to sit down."

Derek smiled slightly. "It does take your breath away."

Reginald stepped up and placed a hand on Derek's shoulder. "Derek, I love you as if you were my own. We will find out who took your mother away from you, I promise. In the meanwhile, don't give Slappy a hard time about what happened between him and your mother. It's in the past and that's where it should stay."

The detective pondered the notion. He was still confused and upset by the whole idea of an affair. To him, his mother was full of purity and innocence. She had a special invitation to Heaven to be the envy of all the angels that frolicked there. To taint that image with the vile conception of an affair was stirring the demons in the pit of his stomach.

He calmed his spirit with the desire for retribution. "I wish I could Uncle Reggie, but it seems that the past is haunting my future. I have to see this through. I need to talk to Slappy."

Reginald patted him on the shoulder as a gesture of approval. "You're a grown man now. Do what you think is right." He nodded as Reginald started for the door. "But just remember who you are dealing with. Slappy will give his life for you."

"I will." he answered.

Derek's surrogate uncle reached the foyer and opened the door. Derek saw Reginald's eyes go wide when he saw the gun pointed at his chest. Michelle Gomez was standing at the threshold. She was a slightly older version of Indy. Despite her sun-bronzed, battle-hardened face, her skin was creamy and smooth. Her military groomed body filled the black outfit in all the right places. She wasn't exactly her sister's equal, but she could have been a model if she tried. However, the ominous smile on her face relayed that her desire to be a model was far from a consideration. It was a smile of vengeance and of satisfaction.

"Good morning Major." she greeted as she cocked the weapon.

The private investigator quickly executed a jump front kick, forcing the pistol to fire harmlessly at the ceiling. The female assassin attempted to re-train the muzzle towards Derek, but he was already on the attack and grabbed her wrist blocking her attempt.

Gomez quickly threw a fist to the face, but Derek stopped that attempt as well and they stood there arms locked. She gritted her teeth in protest as Derek took the opportunity to twist her wrist and force the gun out of her hand. She grunted and sent a side kick catching Derek in the stomach. The blow caused the investigator to stagger backwards, doubled over and fighting to catch his breath.

He looked up to find the female soldier coming in for an attack. She suddenly staggered sideways and slammed hard into the doorframe after receiving a punch in the jaw from Reginald. Her eyes flashed vengeance as she sent a heel towards his chest. The surrogate uncle caught the foot only to leave himself wide open for a jump crescent kick. His body quickly spun to the ground.

Derek saw his opportunity and took two steps before jumping in the air with a jump sidekick catching Michelle Gomez square in the back. She hit the foyer wall face first. She retaliated with a spinning back fist, but Derek ducked the attack and countered with a punch to the kidneys. She grunted from the attack and sent her foot backwards catching him in the groin. A tear rolled from his eye as he fell to one knee. She turned and sent a foot to his chin sending him face first onto the floor.

He lifted his head to find the blurred image of Michelle Gomez moving her dark mane from her face and picking up the discarded pistol. "You fool." she said as her image cleared. "You're not *my* target."

He watched her cock the weapon as a shot rang out. Michelle Gomez's eyes became glassy and he could tell that she was trying to comprehend what had happened.

She fell to her knees as blood frothed from her lips. Indy's image replayed in his mind like a bad drive-in movie.

Blood started to pool around the female soldier's body as Derek slowly rose. He looked to find his surrogate uncle placing his gun back in its holster. "Who the hell was that?" Reginald asked as he clasped the holster strap.

"Michelle Gomez."

Reginald rubbed his jaw and gave a quick hunch of his shoulders to straighten his suit jacket. "Tough bitch."

Derek stretched his neck out as he reached for the cordless phone on the console table and dialed 911. For the VBPD's Forensics team, it would be the fourth time in two months that they were his houseguest. The first time, they were picking out bullets from his front door, the second and third time consisted of expelling the house of corpses. Austin would not be pleased with the removal of a third.

"Who are you calling?" the FBI agent asked.

"The police. This will be the third body bag removed from this house in two months."

Reginald snickered. "And I thought I had a problem with mice."

<u>**Chapter Sixteen**</u>:

The black private investigator was usually unaffected by the smell of designer hair grease, but this time it was different and unsettling. Butterflies danced in his stomach and his mouth was dry. Slappy was like a second father to him, but Slappy had lied to him. Whatever bond they had formed over the years had been ruptured in that one instance. Derek needed an explanation, and he was determined to get it.

A new track from Busta Rhymes reverberated across the walls of the barbershop. The barbers and patrons alike were bobbing their heads to the heavy bass and the lyrical tirade of the hip-hop artist. They were having a good time, unaware of their employer's deception and Derek's true reason for being there.

He found Slappy in his usual spot tending to a customer. The older barber and proprietor was in tune with the music as he bobbed his head with a smile. He gave a nod when Slappy looked up and waved him over. The private investigator took in a deep breath as he frantically searched for an opening statement.

"Your two love birds are in back." Slappy began. "You may wanna knock, because when I last checked, they were still kissin' and huggin'. I think they were up all night. Tell you what? There better be some clean sheets on my couch. White folks havin' sex in a black man's bed, what kinda mess is dat?"

Derek ignored Slappy's comment. "May I talk to you?"

"Can't you see that I am cuttin' someone's hair?"

His voice seemed more stern, almost parent like, as it dropped a few octaves. "I need to talk to you now."

Slappy stopped grooming his patron and read Derek's eyes. The black private investigator was serious. He placed the electric clippers down and started for the back room. "Okie dokie. Let's talk."

Derek followed him to the employee break room where he found Mallott and Mrs. Cooke in a passionate embrace. Slappy cleared his throat to announce his presence. Mallott and Mrs. Cooke quickly parted and tidied themselves.

"Mallott," Derek began. "Please take Mrs. Cooke to the front entrance and wait for me."

Mallott stood up from the couch and made a gesture to his pink robe. "Sure, but can we please stop at a store so I can pick up some clothes? I haven't showered for two days and I'm feeling a little sleazy."

"You are sleazy." Derek retorted. "Please take Mrs. Cooke up front. I will join you shortly."

"I need to look good for my lady." Mallott added.

The detective grabbed him by the collar. "I won't ask again. Please take Mrs. Cooke up front."

Mallott nodded quickly as Derek released him. "C'mon Doll-face, let's blow this popsicle stand."

Mrs. Cooke stuffed her belongings, namely lipstick, eyeliners and a hairbrush back into her diamond studded purse and quickly followed after her lover. Slappy looked at Derek with bewilderment.

"So, what's so damn important that you had to get off your chest right here and now?"

Derek yelled as he sent a fist across Slappy's jaw. The blow sent the proprietor of Buzz Cutts staggering backwards causing him to crash into the break room table. It toppled over sending Slappy and discarded dishes onto the floor.

"You sonovabitch!" Derek shouted. "You lied to me!"

Slappy slowly rolled to his knees. "Lied to you about what?"

"My mother!" Derek yelled. A tear was forming in his eye. "It *was* you who had the affair!"

Slappy took hold of the kitchenette counter-top and slowly stood to his feet. He turned to face the detective as Omar stepped into the doorway. He was soon joined by the other barbers. Each looking on with confusion. Slappy held his hand up. "It's okay fellas. Handle your business. I got this one."

They stood there looking on wondering how the scenario would play out.

"I said get back to your stations!" Slappy ordered.

They looked at each other and then back at Slappy before they slowly vacated the doorway. Omar stood rigid, but Slappy waved him out. Omar slowly disappeared from the doorway. Derek respected the barbers for their loyalty to the proprietor, but he would gladly go through them if he had to.

"Why Slappy?" Derek asked. "Why did you lie to me?"

Slappy chuckled quietly as he rubbed his jaw. "Your mother made me promise not to say a word to anybody, especially to her children. I'm sorry for what happened. It wasn't supposed to, but I loved your mother."

"Did you kill her?"

Slappy's resolve began to rebuild itself. "You must be out of your damn mind! No, I did not kill her!"

"Your commanding officer seems to think otherwise."

"My commanding officer?" Slappy asked mainly to himself. "Janocky? Janocky told you that?"

"He believes that the person who had the affair with my mother is the same person who killed her."

"Janocky is also the crazy sonovabitch that put my ass in a firefight that should've never happened. If I was going to kill anybody, it'd be him."

"I don't believe you."

Slappy took in a deep breath and wiped the stream of blood from his lips. He looked at the son of the man who saved his life. He shook his head and smiled with satisfaction. "Master Roo taught you well. You've gotten faster." Slappy sighed as he flopped down in a chair. "Derek, the truth is that your mother always loved your father. It was a moment of weakness for the both of us. It was an affair that lasted less than a week. We saw each other twice, although it should have never happened in the first place. At first, we were really careful. We went up to this empty cottage near La Cabra. Then one night we got full of ourselves and Reggie saw the whole thing. He told your father. The morning she died, your mother, your father and myself sat down and we talked. Your father's first response was to whoop my ass. Who could blame him. I'd do the same thing if I was in his position; but your mother convinced him otherwise. She even made him promise to be civil to me. I promised your father that I would leave for the states in the morning and would never be an intrusion in his life ever again.

"When I heard the news of the accident, your father and I both lost someone we loved. It was the grief we shared that helped us to remain friends. Is he still sore at me?" Slappy asked. He raised an eyebrow as his tongue probed his cheek. It was assessing the damage from Derek's punch. "I reckon he'd still whoop my ass if reminded."

"If you were that broken up about the affair why didn't you leave right away? Why did you wait until morning?"

"If you must know, I was there at the request of the State Department. So was Reggie. They were building a case against Janocky."

"The government was building a case against Janocky?"

Slappy nodded. "Oh yeah. They were going to court martial him the day of your mother's accident."

"Uncle Reggie didn't mention anything to me about that."

"He didn't?" Slappy asked. "That's strange. The State Department needed our testimonies regarding the firefight in Vietnam."

"So you both were at La Cabra during the accident?"

"Yeah," Slappy answered. He then stopped as his mind replayed the events of that day. "Actually, I take that back. They didn't get Reggie's statement until later."

"How much later?"

"I'd say Reggie showed up about an hour after I did. A jeep dropped him off at the front gate. Said he was late because the rental car we had was having engine problems." Slappy gave a humpf. "Funny. It was a new Datsun and it drove just fine for me. It shouldn't have had any problem at all."

Derek's face turned rigid as he processed Slappy's information. "Uncle Reggie showed up an hour after you got there?"

"Yeah." Slappy answered. "Why?"

"He said you two were together."

"Nope," Slappy replied. "I took one of the local taxis up the mountain that day. Reggie said he had some errands to run." The barber then paused and contemplated what Derek was thinking. His expression confirmed Slappy's suspicions. "You can't really be serious? You think Reggie killed your mother?"

Derek could feel his heart thumping against his chest and the pit of his stomach churning. He felt sick. "I'm not sure what I'm thinking."

"What possible motive could he have? Why on earth would he kill Kara?"

"I don't know."

"It doesn't make sense."

Derek looked at the barber with exasperation. "Nothing makes sense anymore! But dammit there's going to be hell to pay when it does." and he walked out of the employee break room.

The ride back to Derek's beach house remained a quiet one. Mallott seemed on edge as he sat in the passenger seat. Mrs. Cooke sat in his lap curled up like a kitten sensing the intensity circulating throughout the car. The only thing that broke the silence was the whirring of the Ferrari's engine as it rumbled down Shore Drive, one of the many strips of road that connected the laid back, resort-like atmosphere of Virginia Beach to the fast paced, city lifestyle of Norfolk.

Mrs. Cooke was the first to speak. "Walty? Do you think the Feds will let me stay with you?"

Mallott shrugged and turned towards Derek. "I don't know. Do you think they'll let her stay with me?"

Derek, still recalling the altercation with Slappy, shrugged as well. "It's up to the Feds. They might, but I doubt it. Mallott's the only one testifying against your husband."

Mallott gave Mrs. Cooke a squeeze. "Don't fret your pretty blue eyes, Doll-face. I'll only testify if they let me take you with me."

Derek sighed.

"What?" Mallott asked. "You still don't believe we love each other? You think she's settin' me up or somethin'?"

The detective smiled sheepishly. "The thought had crossed my mind. It was quite a coincidence that a couple of Cooke's blockheads just happen to follow her over to Wesleyan. Let me ask you something Walty? Did you call her from your hotel?"

Mallott nodded. "Of course. I wanted her to know that I was okay."

Derek gave a nod and quickly jerked the steering wheel towards the sidewalk pulling the car over. The Ferrari then came to an abrupt stop. Mallott tightly held onto Mrs. Cooke, but her face slapped the dashboard. Her body quickly bounced back into Mallott chest.

"Ow!" she whined. "That hur-

Derek's fist recoiled from Mrs. Cooke's painted face. Her eyes rolled up in the back of her head as she slumped over Mallott's shoulder. She laid there unconscious and Mallott instantly went into a rage.

"Why the hell did you do that?"

Derek grabbed Mallott by the ear and tugged. "Listen you moron. For the last time, she is setting you up. The day I picked you up at the hotel, the only people who knew you were there was myself and the lawyer trying to put your boss away. Remember the two men at Wesleyan? Did you forget that they were the same two men at the hotel? I doubt those two Neanderthals have ESP. Hmmm. Could it be that Mrs. Cooke, Doll-face as you so lovingly call her, dropped a dime on you?"

Mallott looked down at his lover. Derek could see the betrayal beginning to register. "Listen Walty," Derek began imitating Mrs. Cooke's voice. "if you want to be taken out, I will end it right here and right now. Otherwise, ditch the broad and move on with your life."

"But she loved me." Mallott responded.

Derek released his ear. "You may think she did, but she didn't. It was all a lie."

"But you don't understand," Mallott said sadly rubbing the pain from his ear. "Even if it was a lie. It felt good to be loved by someone. She was the only one who ever showed an interest in me."

Derek inhaled and exhaled with a sigh. Mallott had finally reached the point of tugging at his heart-strings. "Walter." began the detective. "I know what it's like to feel rejected, and the excitement of finding that one person that truly wants to spend every waking moment with you, but believe me man, there will be others. There's always others. Just remember to be yourself. No secret agent bullshit or over-the-top Casanova. Let them love you for who you are." Derek then placed the throttle in first and revved the engine. "Now ditch her and move on with your life. Your *new* life."

Mallott took one last look at Tony Cooke's wife. He kissed her on top of the head and opened the door to the Ferrari. "Sorry Doll-face."

Derek watched Mallott gently slide out of the car and carry Mrs. Cooke to a bus stop's wooden bench. The federal witness took one last look at her before hopping back in the Ferrari. Mallott buckled his seatbelt and his cheeks puffed out as he exhaled with a sigh.

Derek chuckled. "She wasn't your type anyway."

Mallott gave him a puzzled look. Derek could tell that he was still denying himself the opportunity to move on. "What is my type?"

Derek smiled as the Ferrari's tires clawed the pavement. "Someone much more attractive and a little less make-up."

The engine to the Italian import purred as it rumbled down Shore Drive. Derek was thinking he could take Shore Drive to Great Neck Road to avoid some of the day's traffic as he took Mallott back to Lynnhaven One. It would be there that Sydney would treat him to a hot shower, a shave, a new Armani suit and a catered lunch. It was her way of showing off for the U.S. District Attorney's office. If they truly knew what Mallott had been through, the U.S. Marshals would be assigned to protect the witness from his protectors.

Derek looked at his watch. He had three hours before Mallott was released into federal custody. His eyes left the hands of the watch and focused on his passenger. His face was melancholy as a result of Derek's abrupt actions of accusing his love interest to be a snitch, before sucker punching her in the face and leaving her at a bus stop a few miles behind them. The detective hoped that despite his measures, Mallott would heed his words and move on to the better life awaiting him.

"You need to trust me on this one." Derek said. "Whether you believe me or not, I did it because I believe there's something better for you. Don't ask me how, but things will be looking up for you." Derek chuckled softly as the words he spoke next

surprised him. "And if the time ever comes when you need me, I'll be in your corner."

Mallott turned his eyes from the scenery of Shore Drive to the driver of the

Ferrari. "Don't do me any favors."

Derek was going to comment before he looked in the rearview mirror and noticed

the armored car coming up beside them. His mind quickly reverted back to the

newspaper article that he read in Sydney's townhouse. He wondered if this was the

vehicle charged with the daunting task of transporting those African diamonds.

His answer quickly came as a black van bounced out of a parking lot in front of

them. It screeched to an abrupt halt preventing them from going any further. Derek

quickly slammed on the brakes as three black-garbed figures exited the van. They

were toting machine guns. The Ferrari skidded to a halt as they fired the guns in the

air.

"Holy sh –

Derek immediately put the transmission in reverse as he heard the wheels of the

armored car come to a grinding halt. The import whined as it started backwards in an

attempt to retreat. The detective turned his head and looked out the back window. The

cars that were following them had stopped and people were ducking for cover. He

spied another black van maneuvering around the traffic and was blocking their escape

route.

Damn! He thought as he saw the doors to the second black van spring open. He

watched four other black-garbed figures exit the vehicle. He jerked the wheel to the right, forcing the Ferrari down West Great Neck Road, a side street that ran parallel with Great Neck Road for about a mile before intersecting with it. He immediately jerked the wheel to the left and the import bounced into the gas station across the street from Seafare Shoppes. The big blue and white sign identified it as Cape Henry Exxon. He briefly remembered the television news story that this establishment and other Tidewater Exxon Retailers participated in the donation of ten thousand dollars to Virginia Beach City Public Schools back in 1998. The money was used to benefit the Kids and College Program. At that moment, the gas station would donate its services and hopefully protect them from an errant bullet.

The car shuddered to a standstill beside a Corvette with a For Sale sign on it and Derek withdrew his Glock as he opened his door. A warm breeze of ocean air filled the interior. "Where are you going?" Mallott asked. "You can't seriously be thinking of taking on these guys?"

His police training was quickly coming to the surface when he answered. "If I don't do something, a lot people are going to get hurt." He could hear sirens in the background. Virginia Beach's finest was quickly on their way to handle the situation. "Stay here!"

Mallott ducked down with a quick nod as the sound of machine gun fire echoed through the air. Derek took the opportunity to leave the protection of the Ferrari and do his part in enforcing the law.

He tactfully darted through the web of parked cars as two police cruisers screeched to a halt behind the van blocking the rear of the armored car. A blue unmarked police car had fishtailed in front of the first black van. The figures in black

garb responded to the intrusion with a bevy of gunfire directed towards the police

officers. Cops were hurrying to get out of their cars and take cover as bullets strafed

the area around them.

A third police car screeched to a halt behind the armored car. He looked to find E

in her uniform opening the door to her cruiser. She crouched down and went to the

rear of her police cruiser as the lights on top of her police car exploded into tiny shards

of plastic. Bullets were searching for a target. She stayed down hoping there would be

some relief to the gunfire. He looked on to find that pedestrians and onlookers were

also ducking behind cars hoping they would be safe from the firefight.

Derek made his way through the crowd and reached the edge of the newly formed

police perimeter. E caught his eye as a bullet punctured the front passenger tire of her

cruiser. Derek hunkered down as E waved him away. He ignored her request and

scurried across to her position. His back slammed hard against the rear bumper of her

cruiser as he took cover beside her.

E gave a huff. "Don't you ever take no for an answer?" she asked. "I said stay

back. Let us handle this one."

"You've been around Austin too long." He snickered. "You're beginning to

sound just like him!"

E smirked as Derek peered over the trunk of the police cruiser. He looked at the

four figures in black at the rear of the armored car. Two of them were kneeling as they fired their automatic rifles at the police. The other two worked on opening the rear door of the armored car.

He ducked down as another bullet ricocheted nearby. "I take it that's the armored car carrying the diamonds?"

E nodded. "It's been monitored since leaving the airport. We're waiting for S.W.A.T. now."

He peered over the trunk of E's car to find another unmarked Crown Victoria pulling up on the other side of the armored car. He raised an eyebrow when he saw Reginald Logan quickly get out of it and run for protection as bullets shattered the Crown Victoria's windshield. Derek's distrust was mixing in with the adrenaline and the desire to see justice.

Bullets strafing the door panels of E's police cruiser forced him to duck back behind the bumper. His police training was swimming through his mind as he cocked his pistol. Ensure the safety of all innocent civilians, secure the perimeter and do everything possible to keep yourself and the suspects alive.

There was a break in the gunfire and Derek and E took that opportunity to stand up and returned fire. He spotted Austin on the other side of the street standing next to his surrogate uncle and FBI agent. Austin was firing his weapon from behind the hood of his unmarked cruiser. The Lieutenant tagged one of the perpetrators in the shoulder causing them to slam against the hijacked vehicle. Austin swiftly ducked for cover as another perpetrator stepped up. They fired at the police Lieutenant laying down cover fire as their fallen comrade crawled for protection.

The back door of the armored car suddenly exploded as a ricocheting bullet sent Derek back behind E's police car. A moment went by before he poked his head out again to find two of the seven perpetrators exiting the vehicle with two metallic briefcases. Sparks flickered over the thieves' heads as bullets from the police bounced off the armored car.

The detective watched as the two figures in black garb surveyed their options. Police had them pinned down and there was no way to secure a vehicle to escape. They gave a nod as they took flight. They ran across the street through the firefight and into Cape Henry Plaza, the home for the Food Lion grocery store and Hot Tuna Bar and Grill, one of the many restaurants labeled as the "locals' favorite". Their five counterparts unleashed the full fury of their automatic weaponry keeping the police from taking pursuit.

"Cover me!" Derek yelled as he moved from the protection of E's police car.

"Derek wait!" E yelled in vain.

Her words quickly faded away, drowned by the exchange of bullets as he sprinted across the street covering his head. He slid over the roof of a parked car and landed hard on the ground just as the windshield exploded above him. He groaned with gritted teeth as tiny pieces of glass rained upon his back. He growled as he sat up. He took in a deep breath and scrambled to his feet taking pursuit of the two fleeing criminals. He had a slim chance of cutting them off. Despite his objective, he was still questioning Uncle Reggie's integrity.

Focus. He thought as he closed in on intercepting the two perpetrators. His pursuit had gone unnoticed and he did not want to inadvertently repeat the scenario at Apollo's Gym. He had to remain focused, because he would be upon them in a few seconds. If his head was not on the situation at hand, his ambush would backfire and he would be good as dead.

He saw an opportunity and leapt onto the hood of a parked Ford Escort. He dove towards the lead perpetrator and tackled him onto the ground. A yelp came from the thief as Derek executed a well-practiced shoulder roll. He was quickly back on his feet as the second thief attacked. The detective cut the attack short with a spinning back kick sending the thief crashing against the door of the Escort.

The first perpetrator sent a leg into the back of Derek's knee knocking him off balance. Derek stumbled forward but quickly steadied himself against the fender of a red sports car. He turned to find the first perpetrator sending one of the metallic briefcases towards his head. He ducked as the silver case cracked the windshield of the sports car. Derek retaliated with a punch to the midsection and a right cross to the face sending the thief staggering sideways.

His attention then diverted to the second perpetrator and his body instantly froze. The second perpetrator withdrew a pistol and was aiming it at his chest. His mind was trying to conjure up a "Plan B" as his adrenaline spiked. However, his racing heart sank to the pit of his stomach when he heard her voice.

"Don't you know it's not polite to hit a woman?"

He seemed confused by the familiarity of the voice. "Courtney?"

Her smile was genuine as she pulled the black ski mask from her head. Like she did so many times in front of the camera, she gave a tilt of her head and swung her hair back into its normal shape.

"You seemed surprised." She said with a smile.

"I don't think surprised is exactly what I would call it."

"Shoot him!" yelled the first perpetrator rising to their feet. The briefcase was still firmly in their grip.

Derek recognized her voice too. He turned towards the thief who tried to hit him with the case of diamonds. "Olivia Lockehart?"

He could see her disgust as she ripped the ski mask from her head. Her usual brown wavy hair was ruffled and did not fall into place as well as her protégé's. "Shoot him and let's be done with this!"

In contrast to the coldness of the muzzle pointed at his chest, Courtney's smile was warm. "I'm sorry Derek. I didn't mean to lie to you."

"So," he began. "The men holding the police at bay with automatic machine guns? Those are Glamour Girls?"

She nodded.

"And the diamond heist in Scotland was your handiwork?"

She nodded again.

"So this whole modeling business is a cover up for an international smuggling ring?"

A giggle almost escaped from Courtney's lips. "You catch on quick."

"Dammit!" Olivia Lockehart yelled. "Shoot him!"

"And your love for me is nothing more than a sham?"

She frowned. "No Derek. It wasn't a sham. I do love you. But in order for me to make this work, I have to be honest with you." She smiled. "There's a lot of things you need to know about me."

Derek raised an eyebrow. "I'm not sure I can handle anything else."

Courtney cocked the weapon. "I'm a United States Customs Agent." She said as the muzzle swiveled towards her modeling mentor. "Olivia Lockehart, you are under arrest for the illegal possession and distribution of international contraband."

He could feel the confusion registering on his face as he watched the same expression unfold for Olivia Lockehart. She stood there frozen. Her look of astonishment slowly resumed to the look of disgust with a hint of betrayal. "You're a Customs Agent?" Olivia Lockehart asked.

Courtney nodded. "Yes I am, and this time, you're going to jail."

Olivia Lockehart took in a deep breath and sat back against the fender of the red sports car. She started to giggle. "Is that so?" She asked with a smile. She then pointed at something over their shoulders. "Please kill them so we can get out of here."

Derek turned as another familiar voice replied. "Sure thing."

His earlier resentment was now rising to the surface. His gut was making sense and confirming all of the evidence he had stumbled across. He now stood face to face with his mother's killer. In addition to the resentment, there was a sudden rush of pain and hurt. It would take all of his objectivity to ask Uncle Reggie why he took his

mother and baby brother away from him.

<u>**Chapter Eighteen**</u>:

Reginald Logan's smile was similar to the smile of someone being caught with their hand in the cookie jar. He took in a deep breath as he held Derek and Courtney at bay with his pistol. "I suppose we should have a talk." Uncle Reggie said coyly.

Derek swallowed hard glancing over at Olivia Lockehart and then back at the special agent. He was beginning to put two and two together. "You're a good liar," he said calmly. "Nobody would ever suspect an FBI agent in charge of tracking down and arresting international thieves to be sabotaging his own investigation at every turn. This missing field agent? Did you kill her because she got too close to the truth?"

"The missing field agent," Courtney spoke up. Her weapon was still trained on Olivia Lockehart. "was Indy."

Derek lowered his head remembering the night she was killed. "Why Uncle Reggie?"

Uncle Reggie shrugged. "Hmm. Should I be a good villain and let you in on the entire plot? Oh hell, why not? Indigo did get too close to the truth and had to be dealt with. While in Paris, she found out that a Customs Agent was also working on the case, but she didn't know who."

Indigo was FBI. Derek thought. *Damn.* He thought back to the night of her seductive striptease and figured it was more than likely a ploy to find out if he was friend or foe. He sucked in his guilt thinking that maybe he should have accepted her invitation. Regardless of his love for Courtney, the gesture maybe would've kept her alive.

"She was a damn good FBI agent." Uncle Reggie continued. "Had a very promising career, so it didn't take her long before she found out about my connection with Glamour Girls and their operation. I couldn't have her ruin it for me, now could I?"

"Shoot them" Lockehart yelled.

"Shut up!" Uncle Reggie replied. "I will deal with them when I am goddamn good and ready."

"When will that be?" Olivia Lockehart asked. There was distrust in her voice. "You said Chase wouldn't be a problem and that you would deal with him. You haven't done shit since this whole thing started."

Uncle Reggie shook his head. The smile on his face was evil. "Has anybody ever told you that you're a real bitch?"

She growled, but it was short lived as he turned the gun on her and fired. Both Derek and Courtney shuddered as the manager of the modeling agency bounced hard up against the fender of the red sports car and fell face first onto the ground. Courtney whirled around, but was greeted by the smoking muzzle of Uncle Reggie's gun.

"Please drop the gun Ms. Lathaye."

Courtney gritted her teeth in denial but complied.

Derek glared at the FBI agent. "The body count just keeps growing huh?"

"A man's gotta do what it takes to survive."

The black detective cocked his head to the side as he processed the information. "Explain something to me. Why kill Indy at my house? Why not during a photo shoot where you could easily pick her off? It didn't seem to stop you when you took a pot shot at me and the models the other day."

"Your house presented the best scenario. Only three people know the code to your father's beach house. You, your father and me. Remember, he was so impressed with it. Said it captured your mother's very essence. It didn't take me long to get him to show me everything. I figured I could use it as a hideout if things ever got too hot, but that idea had to be thrown out when you decided to live here. As for taking a pot shot at you, that wasn't my idea, nor did I pull the trigger. That order came from Diego himself."

"Diego Tosillio?" Derek asked. His heart was pounding against his chest as the anger burned inside the pit of his stomach. The butterflies he had changed to a venomous adrenaline that he was looking forward to releasing.

Uncle Reggie laughed briefly. "Oh yeah, he's the one pulling all the strings. Who do you think sent Indy's sister, Michelle Gomez after you? Yep, that's the way

Diego works. Send two people to accomplish one task, just in case the first person fails."

"Are you sure it was Gomez?" Derek asked. "If I remember correctly, Gomez deliberately tried to kill you at the beach house. She said I wasn't the target."

"Yes, she did say that." Uncle Reggie nodded. "She must've found out that I killed her sister. After all, she and Indy were extremely close." The FBI agent sighed. "I suppose that muscle-bound, bozo of a boyfriend must've told her."

Derek shook his head. "He never got the chance. Someone killed him right after I told him about Indy. I also know how close Indy and her sister were and I seriously doubt Gomez was behind her boyfriend's death." The private investigator smiled as he voiced his speculation. "Sounds like I'm not the only one, Diego Tosillio is after."

The FBI agent laughed with cockiness. "Let him come! He needs these diamonds to finance his operation. If he kills me, he'll never see them."

Courtney spoke up. "You'll never get away with this."

Uncle Reggie shook his head. "I'm already getting away with this!"

Derek swallowed another lump in his throat. It was time to know the truth about his mother. "Did you kill my mother?"

Uncle Reggie took in a deep breath. His face briefly displayed a tinge of regret. "I'm sorry Derek. I was doing my job."

He resisted the anger swelling inside, but it would not be long before he'd lose control and it surfaced. "You sonovabitch! Why did you take my mother away from me?"

His surrogate uncle sighed. "I wish I never accepted all of that money in the first place. Your mother became an innocent pawn in this entire gauntlet."

"That day you and Slappy went to see Janocky, you were an hour late. The sports car you rented? You used it to run my mother and my baby brother off the road. Why Uncle Reggie? You and my dad went to high school together, served in Vietnam together. He saved your life! My dad trusted you!"

It was Uncle Reggie's turn to swallow hard. "I'm sorry Derek. To be frankly honest. I loved your mother too. She was absolutely beautiful. When I found her and Slappy that morning, I was upset." Uncle Reggie continued on with a growl. "Dammit! I was pissed! I told your father, but his love for your mother blinded him of the fact that she was a whore! Only a whore would sleep with her husband's best friend!"

"My mother was not a whore you bastard!"

Uncle Reggie smiled as he shook the gun towards Derek. "Oh yeah, your mother was a whore alright! When the town courier sent me Diego's orders, I'll admit I was more than happy to follow them. But, seeing the tears in your mother's eyes...." His surrogate uncle stood silent for a moment and took in a deep breath. He straightened his posture in defiance of his emotions. "I did what I had to do. Everything was going so well. Diego got what he wanted and I got rich."

"So," Courtney began. "Now you're gonna kill us?"

Uncle Reggie smiled as he cocked the weapon. "Can't take the risk of you stopping me."

The FBI agent suddenly staggered forward as the gun in his hand fired harmlessly skyward. Derek looked past his shoulder to find a man in a pink robe standing behind the special agent. Derek took a step forward hoping to seize the opportunity, but Uncle Reggie stopped him in his tracks by refocusing the muzzle on Derek's chest. The turn-coat FBI agent quickly looked behind him and grabbed the collar of the pink robe. He yanked Mallott forward joining the pink robed interloper with his captive audience. He shook his head as Courtney steadied the federal witness and kept Mallott from crashing into her.

Uncle Reggie smiled as he shook his head. "Well, if it isn't the Whitebread. What the hell were you thinking? Trying to be the hero or something?"

Mallott shrugged realizing his action did not go as planned. His voice trembled slightly. "Trying."

Derek gave a huff. "I thought I told you to stay in the car?"

"I got bored."

Derek gave him a stern look. "Don't make me kill you."

Mallott glared back at him. "Looks like we're gonna die anyway!"

"Shut up!" Uncle Reggie yelled.

A shot rang out and Uncle Reggie's eyes went wide. He looked down as his hand clutched at his chest. There was red liquid covering his fingers. He looked terrified as he looked ahead at the person who shot him.

"You shut up." Olivia Lockehart said with her last breath. She fought to keep her head and the gun in her hand up, but they quickly succumbed to gravity and limply bounced against the pavement of the parking lot.

Uncle Reggie released the gun and the briefcase as he fell onto his knees. Gravity was slowly dragging him toward the same path taken by Olivia Lockehart, but he was caught by the detective before making impact with the ground.

"Uncle Reggie!" Derek yelled as he cradled the man he once trusted. "Uncle Reggie!"

Uncle Reggie fought to speak and grabbed onto Derek's shirt sleeve. He pulled and gestured Derek to lean closer. The detective complied. "Derek...I.....I'm...so sorry."

"Uncle Reggie!" Derek gritted as the FBI agent's eyes fought to stay focused. They were slowly rolling back into his head. "Dammit Uncle Reggie, don't you die!" He said, not really understanding why he said it. He was holding the man who had taken his mother and his baby brother from him, betrayed his father and his family, and would have killed him if the opportunity had played out differently. Derek swallowed hard, half believing that despite all else, he and Reginald Logan had a bond that went further than circumstances.

"Your mother..." Uncle Reggie spat out. "she's...alive."

A tear welled up in Derek's eye trying to comprehend what was being said. "My mother?"

Uncle Reggie coughed. His grip tightened against Derek's shirt sleeve. He fought to keep his eyes open. "I didn't….have…. the heart….to kill….them."

"My mother's alive?" Derek repeated. "Where is she? Dammit Reggie where's my mother?"

Uncle Reggie gagged as he desperately tried to continue. His words were hurried. "He's....coming for you." He warned. "It's not…over."

"Who?" Derek asked shaking Uncle Reggie's body in hopes of keeping him alive. "Diego? Who's coming for us?"

The surrogate uncle took one last breath before his body went limp. Derek shook his body denying Uncle Reggie's fate. After a moment, his efforts to revive his father's best friend ceased and the tear that welled up in his eye rolled down his cheek. The so-called assassin that disrupted his family was now laying in his arms in a gathering pool of blood. It was a terrible and unfortunate price to pay, but came nowhere close to provide a full restitution.

Despite the warning that there was someone else out there patiently waiting to implement his demise, his thoughts were of family and of hope. Of course, the confusion that encircled him was overwhelming. For so many years, he was led to believe that his mother and baby brother were murdered only to discover that they were alive. They were alive! His objective attempts to make sense of everything were challenged by the vast waves of emotional questions. Where were they? Were they in danger? Why had they not contacted him, his sisters or his father? He fought back the tears, but inside he was crying. The type of cry that only a mother's love could fully attend to.

<u>Chapter Nineteen</u>:

In his Armani suit, Mallott looked like a business executive rather than a retired used car salesman in a pink bathrobe. "Thank you for reminding me about who I really am." Mallott said as he shook Derek's hand.

The detective smiled. "Thank you for saving my life."

The federal witness shrugged him off. "Nah. I didn't do anything."

"Sure you did," Derek replied. "If it wasn't for you, I might not be here to see you off."

Mallott turned looking over his shoulder at the two United States marshals standing in front of Saundra's desk. Even with their casual attire of short sleeve polo shirts and jeans, their black rimmed shades and their holstered pistols made them look ominous. Although, they gave an occasional smile or nod, their gestures did little to change that threatening image. It was a good image to have since these men would see that Mallott was safe and secure in his new life.

The door to Sydney Taylor's office opened and she walked up with a manila case file in her hand. She smiled and handed it to Mallott. "Mr. Mallott. This is our file regarding your case. When your trial has concluded and upon entering the witness protection program, that file will need to be destroyed. Do you understand?"

Mallott took the file and nodded. He shook her hand and smiled. "Understood. Thank you for your help."

Sydney shook her head. "No thanks needed."

"Still." Mallott continued. "If it hadn't been for you, who knows where I might have ended up."

Derek chuckled. "I'm sure you would've figured everything out sooner or later."

A cough from one of the marshals broke up their farewells. Mallott looked over his shoulder and gave a nod. When he turned back to Derek and Sydney they could see the sadness in his eyes. "Well, it's time for me to go now." he said. He gave a half-hearted smile. "Maybe one day, we can all get together again. Do lunch or something."

Sydney smiled back. "Maybe one day."

Mallott smiled and walked over to join the marshals. Derek and Sydney watched him as he walked out of Garrett and Taylor with hopes that his new life would be a promising one. Derek took in a deep breath as the glass door with the law firm's marquee closed behind him.

"Don't tell me you're gonna miss that guy?" Sydney asked.

Derek cocked his head to the side. "I can't really say that I will," he answered trying to remember the chaos Mallott had put him through. "but you never know."

Sydney smiled with a humpf. "Why Derek Chase, could it be that underneath that bad ass, playboy image you try so hard to project, there's a warm, caring, soft side?"

The detective took his queue to straighten his posture. He grinned. "Yes, I do have a soft side." he replied. "And she's waiting for me to get back."

Sydney folded her arms with a smirk. "I suppose you would like the rest of the day off?"

Derek raised an eyebrow. "I was actually hoping for the rest of the week."

Sydney's smirk disappeared and her face became serious. She then lowered her head and shook it. "I'll tell you what," she said returning her gaze upon him. There was a smile on her face. "We are getting the case files under control, so you don't have to come into the office, but leave your pager on in case I need you."

He smiled. "Thanks Sydney. I owe you one."

Sydney gave a sheepish grin. "You know Tessa would have never put up with this. You owe me more than you think."

He took the moment to scamper over and kiss her on the cheek. She seemed surprised at the gesture. "Put it on my tab." he said and he quickly made his exit from the office leaving Sydney dazed and confused about her decision.

The warmth of the morning sun soothed his muscles as he concluded his morning Kata. He bowed out of respect and gave one last stretch before looking over at his visitor sitting on the wooden stairs leading to the deck of the beach house. She was wrapped in the blanket that comforted them through the night. Four days had

passed since she told him that she was a United States Customs Agent. Each day and

night they spent together was used to remember old times, catch up on present events

and make love. She became more beautiful and he grew closer to her with each day

spent.

He joined her on the stairs and she opened the blanket inviting him to cuddle with

her. He happily accepted. The warmth of her naked body was comforting against his

bare chest. She squeezed him gently as a sign of affection.

"We can stay here like this all day." she said.

His fingers ran through her soft hair. "I wish we could, but we can't. I need to

see this through the end."

She sighed. "You cared for him?"

Derek kissed her on top of the head. Today, he would bury his surrogate uncle.

"No matter why he did it, he was still like a father to me. It's taking everything I have,

but I have to remember the good."

"Will your father be there today?"

"No." he answered. "My sisters are still trying to get a hold of him. He's still off

on some business trip somewhere."

"I wonder how he's gonna take it."

Derek sighed. "If I know my father, he's not gonna take it too well. He might fly

off the handle and do something rash, like fly to South America and take on Diego by

himself."

"You think he'd do that?"

"It's what I would do if something ever happened to you."

Courtney looked up at him. There was innocence in her hazel eyes. Her innocence soon turned into a halfhearted smile. "You forget who you're talking to. I'm Agent Lathaye. United States Customs. I think I can take care of myself."

"Yeah, I know." Derek chuckled. "You're a regular 007."

Courtney re-nestled herself into his chest. "You better not forget it either."

He took in a deep breath of the ocean's morning air, it smelled sweet and salty. He watched the seagulls frolic nearby. Again, he kissed the top of her head. "United States Customs, huh? So tell me again why the modeling thing didn't work out?"

She giggled. "Oh, but it did work out." she answered. "For three years I was on the cover of some pretty big magazines and a few calendars, but there was no reward in it. Felt like I needed a purpose. I took a few law courses, met this Customs agent during a job fair and he talked me into it. He's now my supervisor."

Derek hugged her. "You didn't sleep with him did you?"

Courtney pulled herself away. "And even if I did, what business of that is yours?"

Derek laughed as he held up his hands in defense. "It's just a question."

"That's some question to ask."

Derek laughed as he removed himself from the blanket. He went down to the last stair and knelt down. He started digging through the sand. "Trust me, I'm full of them today."

"What are you doing?" she asked trying to get a better view.

His heart raced when his finger scraped the wet, sandy velvet of the box. He clawed at it and yanked it from its sandy grave. He opened it and presented it to her. He swallowed hard and took in a deep breath. "I just wanted to make sure that when I ask that special someone to marry me, there'll be no objections at the wedding."

Tears formed in her eyes as the ring sparkled in front of her. "Derek?"

"Courtney Lathaye," he began taking the ring out of the box. "Since the day I met you, I've always loved you." He swallowed hard hoping he didn't stumble over the words that were about to leave his lips. "Will you marry me?"

She wiped a tear from her cheek as she nodded feverishly. "You didn't even need to ask. Yes!"

His heart thumped frantically against his rib cage. A tear was forming in his eye as he gently placed the ring on her finger. She gave a quick glance at it before she was racing into his arms and kissing him. The blanket draped loosely behind her as he cradled her waist.

He gave one last thought about the promise he made to himself about keeping love at bay before sending it to the deepest recesses of his mind. "I love you." he said.

"I love you too."

<u>**Chapter Twenty**</u>:

He took in a deep breath as Reginald Logan's casket slowly made it's descent into the ground. The stripes of the American flag draping the casket waved gently as a stiff summer's breeze cascaded by. The bugle playing "Taps" echoed throughout the cemetery. Derek said a prayer of forgiveness realizing that Uncle Reggie's deceit would remain a secret to the public. He would be buried as an FBI agent killed in the line of duty.

The butterflies in his stomach danced, but were calmed by Courtney's gentle squeeze of his hand. He looked at her and smiled hoping that would reassure her that everything was okay. He returned his gaze upon the coffin as it settled into its resting place. A florist with a large wreath walked up and sat it beside the other flower arrangements. The florist then took off his cap and lowered his head out of respect. He then gave a nod, placed the cap back on his head and walked off back to the white van with the Norfolk Wholesale Florist logo.

The few attendees present slowly departed from the gravesite. He looked across the grave to find E and Austin standing side by side paying their respects as well as being there for Derek. He appreciated the gesture.

He stood there as Slappy stepped up beside him. Courtney saw her opportunity to make her own departure. "Give me the keys, I'll go warm up the car."

Derek gave a nod and extracted the keys to the Ferrari from his suit pants. They dangled briefly before Courtney took them. She kissed him on the cheek and whispered in his ear.

"Take all the time you need. I love you."

He gave a nod as she kissed him on the cheek again before departing. He gave a glance at Slappy who was staring into the abyss of dirt. "You okay?."

Slappy exhaled and forced a smile. "I never wanted this to happen. I'm sorry."

"I know."

"I know things may change between us." Slappy explained. "But I want you to know that I love you. You are like a son to me. I promise there will be no more secrets."

"I know Slappy." Derek replied as he watched E and Austin make their way over. He caught Austin's quick glance at the flower arrangements. His eyes followed the police Lieutenant stepping over to the wreath that had just been delivered and pulling the card from its floral arrangement. "No more secrets."

"So she's alive?" Slappy asked.

Derek nodded.

"Do you believe him?"

He swallowed the lump in his throat one last time before thinking about his mother. "It doesn't matter if I believe him. I have to hope that he was telling the truth and that she is alive."

He and Slappy started their departure and was soon joined by Lieutenant Austin and E. Austin handed the card from the wreath to Derek. "Chase, I'm sorry for your loss. I heard he was a good man."

The detective gave a nod of approval as he opened the card. "Thanks Lieutenant."

"If you need anything," E added. "Just give me a call." And she kissed him on the cheek.

Derek forced a smile. "I will. Thanks E."

"You know Chase," Austin began. "I told Ms. Companstella that I would take her to lunch down at the oceanfront today."

E looked at him with confusion. "You did?"

Austin gave her a quick nod as he continued his deception. "Why don't you come join us?"

"Thanks, but that's okay," Derek answered as he began reading the note. "Maybe some other time."

Austin gave a shrugged. "Okay, we'll do that. But don't expect my generosity to last forever."

Derek ignored Austin's last comment as he read the note. His stomach tightened. It read: ***I'm coming for you Derek Chase...***

He heard the familiar sound of the Ferrari coming to life and looked up just in time to see its hull buckle as a deafening roar echoed through his ears. His body was suddenly blown backwards by a wave of heat. The wind was knocked out of him as he landed hard on the cemetery lawn. It seemed like everything was moving in slow motion as he fought to regain his breath. He looked around to find that Slappy, E and Austin were also recovering from the sudden jolt. Suddenly, looked towards the Ferrari realizing the horror of what transpired. He yelled her name, but the constant ringing in his ears prevented him from hearing it.

"Are you trying to excite me?" Derek asked with a sheepish grin.

She smiled at his flirting and chose to engage it. "If I was trying to excite you, your pants would be to your ankles by now."

He rubbed his thin goatee and looked down at his black suit pants. He smiled contemplating her remark. "That could still be arranged."

She smiled shaking her head. "You're terrible. Don't you have a girlfriend?"

"Nope," He answered in what could be taken as a jubilant cheer. "My little black book has more lives than a litter of kittens."

"There must be someone out there," she asked.

"I'm sure there is." He responded with a sheepish grin. "Unfortunately, she doesn't know it yet."

He quickly scampered to his feet and took a step towards the incident in front of him, but his body was held back by Austin. He could faintly hear the Lieutenant's voice as Austin held him at bay. "Chase, you can't!"

"So where do we go from here?" she asked.

He raised an eyebrow. "You tell me," he replied. "Was last night something that you felt, or just a roll in the hay with an old classmate?"

She looked at him. "That sounds a little harsh," she said. "I like to think of last night as something special."

He looked at her, searching for some truth in her brown eyes.

She replied to his silence. "I woke up this morning feeling something I haven't felt for a long time. I often wondered what it would be like when we saw each other again. I will admit that when I left to pursue my modeling career, I was running away. I was scared and in doing so, I ran away from my feelings and the one person who meant more to me than anything else." She smiled at him as she placed the coffee mug on the wooden stair. She then lovingly cupped his hands. "I love you too. I've never stopped loving you."

"No!" He yelled. "Courtney!"

"What are you doing?" she asked trying to get a better view.

His heart raced when his finger scraped the wet, sandy velvet of the box. He clawed at it and yanked it from its sandy grave. He opened it and presented it to her. He swallowed hard and took in a deep breath. "I just wanted to make sure that when I ask that special someone to marry me, there'll be no objections at the wedding."

Tears formed in her eyes as the ring sparkled in front of her. "Derek?"

"Courtney Lathaye," he began taking the ring out of the box. "Since the day I met you, I've always loved you. Will you marry me?"

She wiped a tear from her cheek as she nodded feverishly. "You didn't even need to ask. Yes!"

His heart thumped frantically against his rib cage. A tear was forming in his eye as well as he gently placed the ring on her finger. She gave a quick glance at it before she was racing into his arms and kissing him. The blanket draped loosely behind her as he cradled her waist.

He gave one last thought about the promise he made to himself about keeping love at bay before sending it to the deepest recesses of his mind. "I love you." he said.

"I love you too."

Little tiny flames rained down upon the earth as tears formed in Derek's eyes. His heart sank as he felt his soul being ripped from him like a discarded page of a book. His curse had once again trumped him. He sank to his knees and cried as he watched the fire happily consume the Ferrari's fiberglass body and extinguish the love of his life.

No!

END